RAINSE

STARLIGHT MERMEN

STARLIGHT ALIEN MAIL ORDER BRIDES
BOOK 9

SKYE MACKINNON

Peryton Press

CONTENTS

To Loki.
Welcome to the family.

GLOSSARY

Eynhallow – a city on Finfolkaheem

Finfolkaheem – planet of the finfolk

Intergalactic Authority (IA) – space police

Intergalactic University (IGU) – the best and biggest university in the galaxy

Mooncrossing – a year on Finfolkaheem

Roussay – a town on Finfolkaheem

Span – a week on Finfolkaheem

Sunpass – a day on Finfolkaheem

PROLOGUE

Verity

I'd always loved whales. Until the day one tried to kill me.

Or maybe it didn't. Maybe it just wanted to play and didn't consider that it was so much bigger than the RIB.

Either way, it hit us like a truck, slamming into the boat from the side. The impact tore through the inflatable's hull with a sound like thunder. There was no time to radio for help. We were in the water before we could blink.

One moment, we were laughing about the playlist Hugo had put on – *Under the Sea*, of all things – and the next, the world flipped upside down. Cold swallowed me whole. The sea punched the air from my lungs, and I barely remembered to close my mouth before the saltwater rushed in. My life jacket yanked me upwards, forcing me to the surface just in time to see the whale's tail fin rise like a mountain behind me, then crash down, sending a wave that rolled me over again.

When I surfaced a second time, coughing and choking, it was gone. Its work was done.

The sea around us was a chaos of foam and debris. The overturned RIB bobbed nearby, half-submerged. The engine hissed and spat before dying entirely.

"Hugo!" I gasped, throat raw from salt and panic.

He surfaced a few metres away, eyes wide, coughing up seawater. "I'm here! Jammie?"

A spluttered reply came from somewhere to my left. Relief, sharp and fleeting. All three of us. Alive. For now.

We tried to stay afloat as the sea rocked us like rag dolls. There was nothing around us but endless blue – no shore, no boats, no sign of rescue. The *Minerva*, our main vessel, had to be out there somewhere, but the swell made it impossible to spot her. The horizon was a jagged line between sea and sky.

I tilted my head back and stared at the sky. A single gull circled high above us, its cry thin and lonely. The world was too vast, too silent, too indifferent.

I'd always loved whales. Their songs, their grace, their impossible size. It's why I had spent my adult life studying them. But floating there, tiny and breakable in the endless ocean, I realised love could be as dangerous as it was beautiful.

Now, we could only wait to be rescued.

Or to become part of the deep.

1

Rainse

Jealousy didn't suit me, and yet I wore it like a cloak. Hiding my envy became more difficult with every day.

The two people closest to me, my clutch-brothers, the finmen I'd grown up with, who I'd travelled all this way to another planet with - they had found their mates and were busy kissing, swooning, disappearing into quiet corners.

But not me.

I was still alone. Every sunpass - no, several times every sunpass, what humans called day - I checked my messages, just in case I'd overlooked a notification from the dating agency. Nothing. How could it be that my brothers had both found a female, yet I hadn't?

It wasn't fair. I hated being alone more than ever. Until we'd come to this planet, at least the three of us had shared our pain, our loneliness. None of us had been given the honour to be allowed a mate. I had almost made my peace with that - until Fionn had heard about this planet, Earth, and we'd gone on the adventure of our lives. For Fionn and Cerban, the risk had paid off. I was still waiting.

And there was no guarantee that I'd ever find a mate here. Out of the twenty-something finmen who'd travelled with us, half had been matched with a human female. Pam, the leader of the Hot Tatties dating agency, insisted that those odds were 'absolutely fabulous' and that she'd never worked with an alien species this compatible with humans.

I seemed to be an exception. While my brothers got to spend time with their mates, gallivanting around with huge grins on their faces, I was left to spend my days working hard to keep the peace between humans and finmen. The job had got easier over the last few spans, now that the two species had got to know each other. Everyone could see how well the matched couples got along - sickeningly so. It churned my stomach every time I saw a finman kiss a human female. Not because of the species difference, but because I craved to be in his position. I wanted a mate with every cell of my being. Jealousy was exhausting.

I didn't have to work this sunpass, but I'd been hiding in my office until a few clicks ago, distracting myself by sorting virtual files and reading news reports from back home. I missed Finfolkaheem. The vast, endless oceans. The underwater cities twinkling like beacons at the bottom of the sea. The food, oh yes, the food. Fish on this planet lacked the flavour I was used to. I had tried other dishes, plants grown on land rather than in the water, but they weren't salty enough. My clutch-brothers embraced the exotic food Peritus offered, but I couldn't be like them. Maybe if I'd had a mate, it would all be easier. She could introduce me to this world, stroke by stroke, until I forgot Finfolkaheem and its delicacies, the taste of its ocean, the scent of its soul. I was sure that everything would be so much better with a female at my side.

I stretched my shoulders, arched my back. I'd been sitting inside for too long. A swim in the sea would do me good and rip me from my maudlin thoughts. The good thing about living on an island was that the sea was never far away. Even if the sea didn't taste quite right.

When I got to the closest beach, I spotted Cerban and Maelis in the distance. She was wearing her diving equipment, he followed behind her like an enthusiastic catfish. I turned away from them, unwilling to see their happiness up close.

I hated the male I'd become. Bitter. Jealous. Full of dark thoughts that I couldn't push out of my mind.

Maybe I should never have come here. Maybe the Matriarchs were wiser than I'd thought. Their system had worked for generations, ever since climate change had increased the water temperatures, causing fewer females to be born. Now only select few males got to have a mate. It was sad for the rest of us - no, not sad, devastating - but now that I saw the male I was becoming, twisted by jealousy, I could understand their reasoning. I wasn't worthy. I didn't deserve a mate.

The cool water welcomed me like an old friend. I dove into the waves, swimming as fast as I could, away from the island, away from my brothers. I breathed in deep, my gills filtering the water, delivering fresh, cold oxygen into my lungs. My greenskin fluttered in the water, measuring the currents, keeping me steady. Schools of fish swam past me, ogling me curiously but without fear. I could sense larger animals swimming in the distance. Since we'd come to Peritus, I'd spent a lot of time in this ocean. I'd met huge beasts in its depths, but I lacked the knowledge of their names and species. The humans had told us about whales and sharks, but I was sure I'd seen other creatures down there, where sunlight didn't reach and the water grew icy cold. Creatures big enough to scare even a finman warrior who had been in the Finfolkaheem navy for a while.

A *short* while. Until I'd refused an order and had been thrown out unceremoniously.

I was tempted to dive down as far as I could. I was in the mood for a fight, even if it was with a sea creature ten times bigger than me. I no longer cared about my safety. I didn't care about anything. All I wanted was for the anguish in my chest to be extinguished. I wanted peace. But would I ever find it on this planet? I was starting to doubt it.

The droning vibrations of a motor made me come to a halt. A ship, a big one. Not many vessels travelled in these waters - one of the reasons why the Hot Tatties dating agency had bought the island. They wanted privacy, no prying eyes, no alien hunters, no governments who might want to experiment on us. For all anyone knew, this was a billionaire's playground, where the rich stayed in fancy beach huts and had their every wish catered to. In reality, this was the only place on this planet where aliens and humans could live in harmony. And soon, there would be a second island, not far from here, for permanent settlements. There was only one small ferry between the agency's island and a bigger one a few hours by sea, with a hospital and larger airport and other amenities.

But this ship sounded bigger than the ferry by quite a bit. What was it doing in these waters? Curiosity felt better than jealousy. I might as well spend this afternoon chasing a mystery.

I changed course, swimming with strong beats of my webbed feet while slowly approaching the surface again. I'd have to be careful not to be seen. My kind was the origin of humanity's legends of mermaid and mermen, but we hadn't swum in these oceans for centuries. By now, legends had become myths, fairy tales that only children believed in. I didn't want to be responsible for their revival. Humanity hadn't officially encountered other species yet. Most of them thought they were alone in the universe. I snorted, bubbles brushing against my lips. If only they knew.

The vibrations shuddered against my greenskin. I was getting closer. The water here was murky, full of tiny particles rising from the deep. Green strands of plant material moved in the current like dancing curtains. I passed a turtle, swimming slowly but steadily, flippers moving in an ancient rhythm. It had been Elise, Fionn's mate, who'd taught me the animal's name. I waved at the turtle. It stared back at me from old, wise eyes.

A dark shape appeared in the distance. The ship's hull. I slowed down a little, unsure of what instruments and scanners the humans would have on board. Would they be able to sense me beneath the surface?

I realised I didn't care. This was distracting me from the mess of emotions wreaking havoc inside my mind. I was going to be selfish.

I circled around the ship, approaching it from behind. Its huge propeller ploughed through the water, cutting it into pieces. I kept a safe distance from the metal guillotine. Beheading wasn't on my schedule for this sunpass. But I wouldn't glean information from down here. A few barnacles covered the hull, and there was a word painted on the side of the ship, but not in an alphabet I could read. If I wanted to know who this ship belonged to and what it was doing so close to the island, I'd have to surface.

From below, I watched the movement of the waves above me until I'd learned the pattern. Then I rose, my head breaking through a wall of water. Warm air hit my skin. I stayed low, only my eyes above the water, and hidden behind the waves. The ship was sleek and shiny, looking like it hadn't done many journeys yet. That matched the small amount of barnacles on the hull. Humans were moving around on the decks, waving their arms, shouting. Even from a distance could I see that something unusual was going on. Some kind of emergency?

I swam closer until I could hear their voices.

"... it's been too long..."

"... they were supposed to be here..."

"... not answering..."

I was glad for my translator implant. While I'd done my best to learn one of their Earth languages, English, the implant amplified the voices and erased all interference. It was clear they were looking for someone. Part of their crew? Or someone else?

One male lifted a strange apparatus to his eyes and slowly turned from side to side. When the device was pointed in my direction, he yelled something.

Time to disappear.

I dived far beneath the vessel until I was sure they wouldn't be able to find me with their primitive sensors. Finfolkaheem technology was far advanced to what they had on this planet, even after the no-tech movement a generation ago.

What to do now? I could swim back to the island. Or I could do something useful with my time and investigate the mystery of this vessel. They were searching for someone, or several someones. I would do the same. It would keep me out of trouble - and my thoughts from straying too close to yet more jealousy and self-pity.

I closed my eyes and listened to the sounds of the ocean. First, the engines of the ship above me, the propeller cutting through water. Then, footsteps echoing on metal. Human voices. Birds screeching high above them. I expanded my senses beyond my immediate surroundings. Air bubbles. Fish moving in large shoals. The turtle from earlier. And then, deep beneath the oceanic orchestra, a slow, sad song. I'd heard it before, sung by a creature as large as a star-eel, moving elegantly through the depths. They were majestic beasts, with large flukes that could easily knock a finman unconscious, and eyes that spoke of intelligence and awareness. They were singing in the distance, but their song was not the same melodic beauty I'd heard the last time I'd encountered the creatures. They sounded distressed.

I stayed in place for a moment longer, listening for anything else that could show me where to go, but my mind kept returning to that sad song. I didn't have any other leads. I didn't have to return to the island any time soon. So I swam, away from the ship, towards whatever awaited me in the deeps.

2

Verity

I was no longer scared. I no longer scanned the waves for the curved dorsal fins of sharks. I was spread out on my back, staring up into the cloudless sky, imagining I was floating in my bathtub back home. The lifejacket steadied me in the waves that pushed me from side to side. My ears were beneath the water's surface, erasing the sound of the gulls screeching high above. *Float to live.* I'd seen the sign on lifeboat stations back home in the UK. I'd never thought I'd have to use that advice myself.

My lips were dry and cracked despite the water all around me. I was thirsty, so very thirsty. The urge to drink was even stronger than the desire to sleep. Exhaustion pulled at me, the desperate need to close my eyes and surrender to the darkness. But I kept my eyes open and watched the gulls. They meant there was land nearby. I hadn't been involved in charting today's course, so I was unaware of any islands that might mean my survival.

Hugo would have known. But Hugo had swum away, unwilling to listen to me. I'd told him that they'd be looking for us at our last known location. If the *Minerva* came looking for us, they'd come in this direction. There was no point in wasting energy trying to swim to them. It was impossible. But Hugo hadn't listened. Now he was gone. At first, I'd watched his slow progress, his head bobbing between the waves. He'd turned and waved a few times, then he'd disappeared in the distance. I hoped he would make it. I liked the guy. He was funny, even if his humour was a little cringeworthy from time to time. His taste in music was atrocious. But he was clever, kind, a nice guy to be around. And he still owed me a round of poker. He better not die.

At least Jammie was still here with me, floating somewhere to my right. He was a PhD student from Birmingham. His thick Brummie accent made me laugh sometimes. He'd begged me to come along on the RIB today. I bet he regretted that now.

In the beginning, he'd asked questions. Would the *Minerva* find us. What if it didn't. What should we do. How could we survive in the middle of the ocean. At some point, he'd stopped asking questions. Whether he didn't like the answers or whether he wanted to conserve his strength, I didn't know.

Despite the silence between us, I was glad I wasn't alone.

The accident kept replaying in my mind. The whale's fluke crashing down on us. The splashing water. Flying through the air, landing in the cold sea. And again, that fluke, waving at us as if saying goodbye. Or maybe 'fuck you, humans, stop bothering me'. It hadn't been one of the whales we'd studied, I was sure of that. I could recognise them all by their dorsal fins, and some had trackers attached to their thick skin to help us trace their movements and understand their behaviour better.

"Jammie, did you recognise the whale?"

My voice sounded as dry as my throat felt.

"No." He coughed. "But... I don't... know them all."

He sounded to be in a worse state than I was in. How long had it been? The one day I'd forgotten to put on my watch... We'd set out in the early morning and had worked for at least two hours, following a pod of minke whales that had come to these latitudes for breeding. They weren't part of my research project, but I'd been happy to spend a day with the other two researchers, helping Hugo record the whales' behaviour and teaching Jammie more about field work. My own research circled around orcas. Most research on them had been conducted in polar and sub-polar regions, which is what I was about to change.

Unless I drowned today. Would anyone continue my studies? Or would it die with me?

That thought gave me renewed strength. It wasn't the whale's fault. I didn't believe that. It had seen us as a threat, or maybe a toy and had reacted accordingly. We had encroached upon its territory, not the other way round. I'd only got a glimpse of its fluke - and I hadn't even seen the whale before it had crashed into our RIB - but I was pretty sure it had been a humpback whale. Just like minkes, they came into these warmer waters to find a mate.

I hoped it would meets its one true love. I didn't wish it ill, not even if this was to be the end.

I was done blaming other people - other whales - for my problems. Even if this whale's actions had been a little drastic.

A bird flew low over our heads. Marine avians were not one of my specialities. To be honest, I could barely tell apart a herring gull from a ring-billed gull. I was all about the cetaceans. My love had started with a cuddly dolphin toy as a child - I bet my grandmother hadn't expected me to make a career out of it.

My chest grew cold at the thought of my family. If the *Minerva* didn't find us, if we...

No. This was not going to be the end.

"Vee..."

Jammie sounded so very weak. I turned my head to look at the young man. He hung heavily in the water; his life jacket was all that was keeping him afloat. If only the RIB hadn't sunk, then at least we'd have something to hold onto.

"Yes?" I croaked.

"I don't... want... to die."

I reached deep for the last remnants of energy and flipped myself onto my front, then slowly paddled towards him. There were only two metres between us, but it felt like miles. I grasped his hand - icy cold - and squeezed it.

"I'm here. You're not alone."

He gave me a grateful smile, but even his smile was weak. His eyes were red-rimmed, salt crusted in his hair and eyebrows. His lips were split open in places. His skin was pale, almost grey. Not good. Did I look just as pitiful?

I turned onto my back again, but kept hold of his hand. The short swim had exhausted me. I had never craved water more desperately.

By the slow walk of the sun across the cloudless sky, I estimated we'd been in the water for at least five hours.

It was afternoon now. And within a few hours, it would be dark. I'd spent enough time on lone ships in the middle of nowhere to know the absolute blackness that would fall over the world once the sun had set. No lights save for the moon and the stars. At least it was a clear day, with no sign of clouds on the horizon. Full moon had been a few days ago, so we'd have enough light to see a shark before it started to eat us.

Sharks were fascinating. And I wanted them to stay as far away from us as possible. It helped that we were floating and not trying to swim anywhere. Neither of us had any injuries save some bruises. If we were lucky, we'd not attract the sharks' attention.

If we were lucky.

I stared into the blue sky and wondered whether I should start to pray. I'd never been religious. Never seen the point in it. I could appreciate a pretty church or mosque or temple as a building, but I'd always lacked the urge to pray to some higher being. Until now. I couldn't save myself from this situation. I was relying on others to come to my rescue. Maybe a bit of divine intervention wouldn't be so bad.

"Vee..."

Jammie's voice was barely audible over the sound of the waves.

"Yes?"

"I can't... hold on..."

I squeezed his hand as tightly as I could. "You will hold on. You-" Water filled my mouth, salt erupted all over my tastebuds. I spat it out, coughing, spluttering.

"You will survive. We both will."

But my words sounded weak even to me. Hope was fading with every passing minute.

Had Hugo made it to the *Minerva*? Or was he lost in the vast emptiness of the Atlantic Ocean? For a moment, I could hear one of the songs we'd sung along to earlier, *Yellow Submarine* by the Beatles. Everything had been okay then. We'd had no idea that less than an hour later, we'd be in the water, fighting to survive.

I started humming the tune. It was a broken, tired attempt, but it gave me something to focus on.

"...mmhm-mmh-mmh-mmh-mhmm..."

Jammie joined in. I looked at him, saw the determination in his eyes and steeled my own will to survive. We could do this. We wouldn't give up.

And that is when I saw the shark's fin cut through the waves. A grey triangle that triggered every single primitive instinct to run, scream, hide. Jammie hadn't seen it yet.

There was nowhere to run. We were sitting ducks.

I squeezed Jammie's hand to get his attention. "Don't move. Don't splash. No sudden moves. There's a shark."

To his credit, he didn't react besides tightening his grip around my fingers. "Hit him... nose?"

"That's what I've heard."

I'd never planned to encounter a shark outside a shark cage.

A shadow passed beneath me. A second shark? It had looked like a smaller shape, but it was gone before I could get a closer look. Not that I wanted a closer look. I wanted to be far away from here, on a safe, dry bit of land.

"Whatever happens..."

I didn't get to finish my sentence.

The fin disappeared, then reappeared a heartbeat later, slicing the water between Jammie and me. The sheer grace of it made my breath catch. Sharks were beautiful — I'd always thought so — but beauty didn't help when you were about to be their dinner.

It circled once. Twice. Close enough for me to see the darker blur of its body below the surface, moving with effortless precision. My heart hammered. The animal was maybe three metres long, smaller than a great white but larger than a mako. A blue shark, perhaps. Common in these waters. Curious, not immediately aggressive.

Please stay curious.

The tip of its tail broke the surface for a moment, glittering in the sun like polished steel. Then it vanished again.

Jammie whispered, "Still there?"

"Yes." My throat ached with dryness. "It's just looking."

He made a strangled noise. "Looking for lunch."

"Not if we stay calm."

It was ridiculous, trying to reason with both him and the sea. I was a scientist, but science didn't comfort me now. Logic couldn't fight teeth. My whole body was trembling, half from cold, half from terror. I tried to focus on the small things: the feel of the current brushing past my legs, the steady up-and-down of the swells, the rhythm of our breathing. If I focused on those, maybe I could pretend this was just another dive, another field study.

The shark came closer. Close enough that I saw the ripple of its gills, the subtle roll of one dark, intelligent eye. It was studying us. Assessing. Wondering whether we'd taste good.

I braced myself. "If it comes near—"

The water exploded beside me.

For one wild instant I thought the shark had struck, but what breached the surface wasn't grey — it was green, shimmering like polished jade. Something — someone — rose from the depths in a surge of power and foam.

Jammie screamed.

I didn't. I couldn't. The sight had robbed me of sound, of thought.

The creature moved with impossible grace. One moment he was beneath the surface, the next he was there between us, chest heaving, water streaming off a body that looked human, but also didn't.

Sunlight caught on him, flashing across the green skin and bits of seaweed attached to his shoulders. His hair was dark, streaked with lighter threads that rippled in the water.

The shark turned sharply and vanished into the blue, as if something larger and far more dangerous had entered its territory.

I hung in the water, frozen. My heart was hammering, too fast to be useful. My brain struggled to form a single rational thought.

He looked at me. Not at Jammie, not at the sea, but straight at me. His eyes were the colour of deep water, shifting and unknowable. They didn't seem threatening, only curious.

He spoke, a sound that wasn't quite human speech but not entirely *other* either. The water seemed to carry it, wrapping the word around me until I felt it as much as heard it.

"You."

My mouth opened, but no sound came out. I was cold to the bone, my teeth chattering so violently I could hardly breathe. Suddenly the last remnants of energy left me. I'd heard about this. People who nearly drowned hung on, only to then go completely limp when they saw their rescuers, believed that hope was imminent.

The world tilted. The sea rushed up again, and suddenly I was moving.

Arms, strong and unyielding, lifted me clear of the waves. I caught a last glimpse of Jammie's pale face as I was drawn against the stranger's chest. He was shouting something, his voice lost to the roar of the ocean. Then the horizon tilted again, and the sky dissolved into light.

Salt burned my throat. My vision narrowed to a single thought.

This isn't possible.

3

Rainse

Nothing had ever felt as right as carrying her in my arms as I swam us to safety.

The waves pressed against us as if trying to take her back. I held her tighter and kicked hard, cutting through the water with strong, even strokes. She coughed once, a weak, broken sound, and her head lolled against my shoulder. The urge to keep her above the surface was so fierce it bordered on pain.

Her scent filled my senses, salt and fear and something underneath, warm and alive. The bond struck again, as sudden as lightning in a clear sky. A pull in my chest so strong I almost faltered mid-stroke. My body knew before my mind did.

My mate.

I'd felt it even before I'd touched her for the first time. I'd heard her voice from beneath the waves, felt the vibrations of her body through the water, and I'd known. She was mine. And I'd finally found her.

I didn't care that my clutch-brothers had taken longer to feel the bond to their mates. I had no doubts that she was the one for me. It was as much fact as breathing.

A flash of memory cut through me: Cerban and the chaos that had followed when he claimed his human. The arguments. The threats from the agency. The endless rules about protection and consent and human rights. They would never allow this. They would take her away, wrap her in safety and study, and I would lose her before I had even learned her name.

I couldn't let that happen.

The nearest islet rose from the sea less than half a league away, a ridge of dark stone surrounded by white sand and green water. I had used it before during patrols, a place to rest and watch the horizon. It would have to do.

I carried her there, lifting her clear of the surf and laying her on the warm sand. A small freshwater spring bubbled up between the rocks near the largest of the trees. At least she wouldn't die of thirst while I figured out what to do next.

She stirred faintly, her breathing shallow but steady. Her body tensed when I shifted her in my arms, a quiet sound escaping her throat. Even unconscious, she flinched at the pressure against her side. My hand brushed something tender just below her ribs and she whimpered, the sound lost beneath the surf. I drew back at once. Bruised, maybe cracked. I would find out when she was awake.

Her skin was cold against my hands. I brushed her hair - the colour of new coral - from her face and felt the fragile beat of her heart through my fingers.

"Live," I whispered. "Please live."

She didn't stir. Her mouth parted slightly, lashes wet against her cheeks. I could feel the mate bond humming between us, faint and steady, calling to me like the moon to the tide. Would she feel it too, once she woke? Or would she be like the other human females, who had to be slowly persuaded and wooed?

I wanted to stay. I wanted to wrap myself around her and keep the world away. But the other human was still out there. The male. I'd seen him drifting before I carried her off. And those sharp-toothed predators might return. They had retreated when I'd approached the two humans, instinctively aware that I was the stronger predator.

Everything in me wanted to stay. The bond pulled at me. But I had a duty. I couldn't let the male drown. It went against everything I believed in, everything I'd sworn when I'd joined the navy.

But I couldn't bring the male here. I wanted time alone with my mate. I had to get to know her, slowly break the news to her that aliens were real and that one of them was her mate. And only once I was sure that she understood the bond between us would I swim us back to the island to introduce her to my brothers and the dating agency. They couldn't do anything once the two of us were mated. Hot Tatties loved rules and paperwork and scientific tests, but they also respected our most sacred traditions. The mating bond was one of them.

The sound of the waves lapping against the islet's rocky shore reminded me that time was of the essence. I had to leave to rescue that male human. I gently touched my mate's cheek, feeling her soft skin against my calloused fingers.

"I will be back soon," I promised. I gathered a few lengths of dried kelp and draped them across her to shield her from the sun and the wind, then slipped back into the water.

I swam as fast as I could. Every moment I spent away from my mate was a wasted moment. When I got closer to where I'd defended the two humans from the sharp-toothed creature, a new sound joined the song of the ocean. The ship from earlier, now slowly approaching.

That made my life a whole lot easier. All I'd have to do was to get the male closer to the ship so they could pick him up and give him the medical attention he surely needed.

He was in bad shape. His breathing was shallow, his eyes closed. Only the air-filled vest around his chest kept him afloat. He'd likely swallowed a lot of seawater, maybe even breathed it in. I knew enough about human anatomy to know that this could be fatal. He needed to be on that ship as fast as possible.

I grabbed the back of his vest and pulled him through the waves, propelling us with strong strokes of my webbed feet. He was heavier than the female - my mate - but still nothing near the weight of an adult finman. I was barely out of breath by the time the ship came into sight.

I didn't want them to see me, so I dived beneath the male and gripped his hips from below, moving him through the water that way. It was slower and more tedious, but I couldn't risk exposure. If they saw me, they might wonder if there were more of me nearby. They could stumble across the dating agency's island and...

No. This was safer.

I was getting too close for comfort to the ship when they finally spotted him. Shouts erupted above us. I held onto him for a little while longer, until I heard the sound of a smaller boat being dropped into the water. He was about to be rescued. I wished him well.

I dived deep, enjoying the freedom of swimming fast. I passed shoals of fish and a few shimmering jelly-creatures, before the change in water temperature told me that I was approaching land.

I angled my body upward again, bursting through the surface into warm, golden light. The sun hung lower now, spilling its glow across the sea in streaks of copper and gold. The air felt heavy with salt and heat, a sharp contrast to the cool deep I'd just left.

The islet wasn't far. I covered the distance in a few strong strokes, driven by the pull in my chest that never quite eased. Every beat of my heart whispered of her, reminding me what waited on that patch of sand.

When I reached the shallows, I let the current carry me the last few lengths. She was still where I'd left her, half covered by the strands of kelp I'd arranged. One had blown to the side. I would find her a better covering soon. Her breathing had steadied; her chest rose and fell in a slow rhythm that soothed something restless inside me.

I crouched beside her and studied her face properly for the first time. Her lips were cracked from salt and sun, her cheeks pale but not ghostly any more. There was a faint bruise on her temple where the waves must have thrown her against debris. Stray strands of coral-coloured hair clung to her damp skin. It was long; when dry I was sure it would reach to below her breasts.

Her wet clothes clung to her. They had dried somewhat in the warm sun, but I should remove them soon, find something dry to cover her with. And then she would need food, water, other essentials. But for now...

A strange peace washed over me. She was safe. My mate was safe.

I reached out and traced the curve of her shoulder with the back of my fingers, light enough not to wake her. Her skin was so soft it startled me. Humans were fragile in a way that made them seem breakable, yet I'd seen her cling to life with stubborn strength. There was courage in her stillness.

A bird screamed overhead, breaking the silence. I looked up, scanning the horizon. The ship was gone now, a faint smudge in the distance. Good. They would have their rescued male and no reason to search further. The ocean would erase all trace of me before they even thought to wonder what else had been in the water with them.

I sat back on the sand and exhaled. The sunpass was warm, the rock beneath me sun-hot against my legs. I could almost believe that the world had stopped turning, that it was just the two of us in the middle of an endless sea.

My brothers would notice my absence eventually. They'd ask questions. But I had time. A few hours, perhaps longer, before anyone thought to look. And by then, I'd have her awake and calm, and maybe she'd start to understand that I meant no harm.

She shifted slightly, a small sound escaping her throat. My greenskin fluttered instinctively, responding to her nearness, the soft pulse of the mate bond thrumming through me. I stilled, afraid to move, watching as her lashes trembled and her fingers twitched against the sand.

Not yet. Let her rest. Let her body recover before I start unravelling her world.

The tide had turned, drawing back from the rocks, leaving tiny pools filled with darting fish. I gathered a few shells and arranged them near her, an old habit from home — offerings of luck and protection. They glittered faintly in the sunlight, colours shifting like the surface of the sea.

My gaze drew back to her wet clothes clinging to her skin. The wind had picked up, carrying a cooler edge, and I knew enough about humans to recognise the danger. Their bodies lost heat too easily. I couldn't delay any longer. But would she understand that I'd undressed her to protect her, not because I wanted to see her naked body?

I hesitated, watching the gentle rise and fall of her chest. She needed warmth more than modesty.

Carefully, I loosened the fastenings of the strange human garments, peeling the fabric away where it stuck to her skin. The wet material was heavy and cold, the smell of salt strong in my nose. I worked quickly, keeping my movements precise, impersonal. This was survival, nothing else.

One day, I would undress her and revel in the moment. I would worship her body and plant kisses on her soft skin. But that was for later.

When the last piece was gone, I rinsed it in a tide pool and spread it on a flat rock to dry. Then I covered her again with the strands of kelp, layering them until only her face and hands were visible. The sun would do the rest.

I brushed a droplet of water from her cheek, unable to stop myself. Her skin had warmed a little, colour returning beneath the pale surface.

That was better.

I lay down beside her, keeping a careful distance, and let the rhythm of her breathing sync with mine. The air smelled of salt and sun-warmed stone.

I should have felt guilt for what I'd done, but I didn't. For the first time in a long while, the ache that had followed me since leaving Finfolkaheem began to fade.

I closed my eyes and listened to the waves.

She was here.

And I wasn't alone any more.

4

Verity

Warmth.

That was the first thing I felt. Not the biting cold I'd expected, but heat seeping into my skin, wrapping around me like a heavy blanket. The smell of salt and seaweed filled my nose. My body rocked slightly, as if the world still moved with the rhythm of waves.

I forced my eyes open. Brightness stabbed at me, evening sunlight bouncing off pale sand and water that shimmered green and gold. The sky above was too blue, too calm, as if the sea hadn't tried to kill me a few hours ago.

I was alive. Somehow.

I tried to sit up and instantly regretted it. My head spun. My throat burned with salt, my lips cracked when I licked them. Everything ached.

A sharp pain shot through my side, deep and sudden enough to steal my breath. I pressed my hand against my ribs, grimacing when even that small touch made me wince. Something had hit me hard out there— debris, maybe. Every inhale felt bruised.

And then I realised I was naked.

The realisation hit harder than the cold ever could. I was covered only by what looked like strands of seaweed — thick ribbons of golden-green kelp draped over me from shoulders to knees. The fronds smelled faintly of brine and sun-warmed rock.

Panic clawed its way up my throat. I snatched at the nearest handful, clutching it tight to my chest. Whoever had done this had stripped me, arranged me like some drowned offering on a beach.

I wasn't alone. I could feel it before I saw him, a heaviness near my shoulder blades.

He sat a few paces away, half in shadow, half in sunlight. For a moment my brain refused to make sense of him. He looked human, almost. Broad shoulders, dark hair slicked back from a face that was too sharp, too still. But his skin caught the light and shimmered faintly green, the colour of deep water. Thin strips of kelp clung to his arms and shoulders, moving with the breeze as if they breathed.

I froze, my breath catching painfully in my chest.

He didn't move, only watched me with eyes the colour of storm glass. Calm, unreadable, far too focused.

My voice cracked. "Who are you?"

He spoke slowly, gently, as if not wanting to spook me further.

"My name is Rainse."

His accent was strange, the vowels drawn out, soft at the edges.

"What..." It felt rude to ask, but it was clear this was the only question that I had to ask. "What... are you?"

"They call me a finman." He said it in the same gentle, soft voice. I had no idea what a finman was, what this was all supposed to mean, but I was going to return to that. For now, I had other, more urgent needs. I could ignore his green skin and kelp-growths and too-pretty-to-be-real face.

"Do you have water?"

He got to his feet in one fast, elegant movement. "I have seen humans drink the juice from this seed. I will bring you proper water later."

He handed me a green coconut. He'd made a hole in the top, giving me easy access to the water inside. I didn't hesitate, drank greedily, cool juice running down my chin.

"Slowly," he said softly. "Don't upset your stomach."

I ignored him and continued to drink until the very last drop. I licked my dry, cracked lips, wishing I had some lip balm handy. Now that my thirst was no longer overwhelming my thoughts, I was ready to ask more questions.

"Where... where am I? What happened?"

His gaze flicked briefly to the sea. "You fell. The water tried to take you. A beast was about to bite you when I intervened."

The shark. I remembered. I gripped the kelp tighter, desperately hoping it was still covering all the important bits. "Did you take my clothes?"

A shadow crossed his face, something like guilt or confusion. "They were wet. Cold. You would not have lived."

I wanted to argue, to demand an explanation, but my tongue felt thick and my body heavy. Logic told me he was right; wet clothing in open air could have killed me. Still, awareness prickled over my bare skin. He had seen me, touched me.

"I should be dead," I whispered.

Rainse looked at me for a long moment. "You are not."

He said it like a fact, not a comfort. Then, more softly, "You are safe."

Safe? Naked? With him - whatever he was? Maybe safe from sharks, but I didn't feel safe at all.

"Where is Jammie?" I asked instead of voicing my thoughts. "He was with me when the shark appeared. He's my PhD student, he-"

"Is he important to you?" Rainse's voice was cool and steady, but I could swear I felt some tension in his words.

"I feel responsible for him. And he's a friend. Not that that's any business of yours. Did you save him as well?"

A small pause. Then, "Yes. He is safe."

"But not here."

He shook his head. "No. Not here."

I looked around me, really taking in my surroundings now that I felt a little steadier on my feet. We were on an island so small that I could see the ocean on all sides. To my right, black rocks reached into the sea, covered in the same kelp that I now had wrapped around me. To my left was a small copse of coarse bushes, not high enough to offer shade from the sun. Behind where Rainse stood, the island rose a little, and sand gave way to grassy soil. Six trees stood haphazardly together, all different kinds - seeds blown here by the wind, lucky to find a spot to grow roots. One of them was a coconut tree. A small spring bubbled among rocks at its feet. I stared up at its lofty heights. Five, six coconuts. That wouldn't keep me going for long - and I'd first have to reach them.

I turned back to Rainse. "Can you get me back to the ship I was on? The *Minerva?*"

My ribs throbbed just from sitting upright, but the question burst out anyway. The thought of staying here another night made the ache feel trivial.

He didn't hesitate. "No. You're hurt. The waves would break you before we reached halfway."

"Why?" I shot back.

He looked out toward the open water.

"The ship is gone," he said simply. "The current has taken it far from here. You are weak. You would not survive the swim."

Something inside me balked at the calm finality in his tone. "Then signal them! You must have—" I stopped myself. What could he possibly have? A phone? A radio? The man didn't even have a shirt.

He shook his head once. "No signal. No need. They found the other one."

The certainty in his voice made the hairs on my arms rise. "How do you know that?"

"I saw them take him," he said, still not meeting my eyes. "He will tell them you are lost. They will look, but not here. This island is not close to the current that would have carried you away, if I hadn't brought you here."

A chill that had nothing to do with temperature crawled up my spine.

"So that's it?" I asked. "You're just... keeping me here?"

"I keep you safe," he corrected softly. "The sea is dangerous. The sun, too. You must rest. You will heal."

"I don't need—" I started, but the world tilted again. My legs gave way, and I dropped to my knees. He was beside me in an instant, steadying me with a touch so careful it made my throat tighten. His hands were warm, strong, the texture of his skin distinctly non-human.

"Slowly," he murmured. "You breathe too fast."

"I'm fine," I lied, trying to pull away. His hand lingered a moment longer before he let go.

He crouched in front of me, so close I could see the faint veins running through the green growths along his shoulders. They weren't kelp after all. They were part of him, moving gently with his breath, alive.

"You need food," he said. "I will find some."

"Wait," I blurted. "You're leaving?"

"Not far." His eyes lifted to the horizon again. "You will see me."

And before I could say another word, he rose and walked straight into the surf. The water welcomed him like a long-lost friend, curling around his legs before swallowing him whole. One blink, and he was gone.

You will see me. As if.

I sat there, clutching the seaweed to my chest, staring at the place where he'd disappeared. A gull cried somewhere above me. The tide sighed against the rocks. Apart from that, nothing. It was utterly quiet.

I looked down at my hands, still trembling. The sunlight glinted on the faint pattern of salt crystals drying on my skin. I should be making a plan—exploring the island, searching for fresh water, building a signal fire. I should be doing something.

Instead, I sat perfectly still, the weight of the kelp heavy on my shoulders, and listened for the sound of the waves breaking differently—proof that he was still there, somewhere under the surface.

He said I was safe.

But safe and trapped felt far too similar.

The moment he disappeared beneath the waves, I was moving.

I didn't have much time. He'd said he wouldn't go far, but "not far" for someone who could breathe underwater might mean half an hour. Maybe more.

I needed to make the most of it.

First: inventory. I still had my life jacket, torn but functional. My clothes were drying on the rocks. No phone—that had gone down with the RIB. No flares. No radio. Nothing useful except my own brain.

Second: options. I could try to signal passing ships, but I hadn't seen any vessels since we'd been stranded. I could attempt to swim to another island, but I had no idea which direction to go, and my ribs protested even the thought of it. I could build a signal fire, but—

I looked around. There were a few pieces of driftwood that looked dry, but if I arranged them into a heap, he'd know immediately what I'd tried to do.

But did I care?

I grabbed the largest pieces and hauled them to the highest point on the island—all of three meters above sea level. My ribs screamed. I ignored them.

Fire. I needed fire. But I had no matches, no lighter, no way to create a spark. The sun was high and bright—could I use my reading glasses? Except I'd left those in my cabin on the *Minerva*, useless as everything else.

"Think, Verity."

Glass. I needed glass. Or something reflective.

The coconut shell—could I use that? No, too curved. The shells scattered on the beach? Too small.

I stood there, breathing hard, staring at my pathetic pile of wood, and felt frustration well up in my throat.

I was a marine biologist with a PhD. I'd survived research expeditions in the Arctic. I'd published papers, secured grants, managed teams. And now I couldn't even start a fire on a deserted island.

A shadow passed over the sun. I looked up to see a frigate bird circling high above, riding the thermals.

Ships. They sometimes followed ships.

I ran back to the beach, searching the horizon. Nothing. Just endless blue in every direction.

But the bird was still circling. That meant something. Land? Fish? A ship?

I grabbed my life jacket and waded into the shallows, waving it above my head. Orange against the blue sky— surely someone would see it.

"Here!" I shouted, even though my voice wouldn't carry beyond the beach. "I'm here!"

I waved until my arms ached. The bird circled once more, then flew off toward the north.

I lowered the life jacket, panting. My ribs throbbed. The sun beat down on my head.

Nothing. No one.

I was utterly, completely alone.

The reality of it hit me like a wave. I sank down into the shallows, salt water lapping around my waist, and let myself feel the full weight of my situation.

I was stranded. Injured. Dependent on an alien who might be my saviour or my captor—I still wasn't sure which.

And the worst part? Some traitorous part of me didn't want to be rescued. Not yet.

I hated that part.

5

Rainse

The sea welcomed me like a heartbeat. It pulsed around me, cool and familiar, washing away the confusion that the human stirred in my chest.

I caught two fish within minutes, slicing through the water with ease and trapping them in my hands. They were small, silver creatures, all bones and salt, but they'd do for now. Humans needed to eat often, or their strength faded.

When I returned to the island, the sun had sunk lower, turning the world to copper and rose. She had fallen asleep, a fragile shape beneath the kelp. Her breathing was shallow but steady. I could still see the faint bruising beneath her ribs, dark marks blooming where the sea had struck her. Humans healed slowly. She would need warmth and stillness for several sunpasses before the pain eased.

I scaled the fish with a shell and placed them on a flat rock near the waterline. Then I remembered that humans didn't eat raw fish. They liked their food cooked or roasted. But I had no fire. Back on Finfolkaheem, I knew which kind of rocks I could beat together to create sparks. Here, I was out of my depth. And there wasn't much dry wood on this islet. Kelp could burn if dry, but it wouldn't sustain the fire for long.

I cursed softly in my own tongue. The sea swallowed the sound.

There was driftwood scattered among the rocks, sun-bleached and dry. I gathered what I could, snapping longer pieces across my knee until I had a pile the length of my arm. I could build her a shelter of sorts, a place to hide from the wind.

By the time I finished, my hands were raw. I sat back and looked at what I'd made — a crude nest of wood and leaves, the beginnings of a camp. The fish still needed cooking.

Her lips were pale, her skin cold to the touch. The sun would sink soon, and once it did, the air would cool fast. Humans lost heat quickly.

She would need fire.

I crouched beside her, running my fingers lightly through the kelp covering her shoulders. It had begun to dry, losing the moisture that had kept it cool earlier. I didn't dare touch her skin again for long — it stirred something I couldn't afford to feel — but I could tell her temperature was dropping.

The agency island wasn't far. I could swim there, unseen, and return before she woke. There would be tools, blankets, maybe even food that wouldn't make her sick.

The thought filled me with guilt and relief in equal measure. I was already lying to her. What was one more secret?

"I will be back soon," I murmured, though she couldn't hear me. "You will not be cold."

The horizon had deepened into shades of violet when I slipped into the water again. The sea was calm, reflecting the first faint stars. I dove deep, letting the current pull me toward the faint lights in the distance — the agency's island, my brothers' new home, the place I'd sworn not to betray.

My chest tightened with the familiar mix of defiance and loyalty. I wasn't stealing from them, not really. I was protecting what was mine. And once I was ready, I would introduce Verity to my brothers and the agency.

I surfaced once halfway there, the line of the island clear against the dusky sky. The air smelled faintly of smoke and oil — the humans cooking their evening meal. I tasted it on the wind, the warmth and salt of it, and thought of the fragile woman lying alone on the sand.

They would call this wrong. Reckless. But I'd spent too many years obeying rules that had done nothing but hurt me.

Tonight, I'd break many of them. And I realised I didn't care. It was for my mate. For her, I'd break all the rules in the universe.

The island glimmered ahead, scattered with lights from the huts and resort buildings that lined the inner shore. I kept to the shadows beneath the water until I reached the quiet side, where the beach curved away from the main settlement.

The air was heavy with warmth and the faint hum of human voices. Laughter drifted across the sand. It should have made me smile, but it only pressed on my chest. That was the sound of belonging, and tonight, I didn't have it.

I pulled myself out of the surf, moving low between the rocks until I reached the line of trees. The sand here was cool, the path to the huts easy to follow.

Fionn's new house came into view first, lit softly from within. I could see movement through the open shutters — him and his mate, Elise, talking over a shared meal. Her laughter carried into the night, light and full of life. The sight steadied something in me, even as it twisted my gut. I was happy for him. I was. But I also knew what it would cost if anyone found out what I'd done.

Kelon, the finman who had financed our trip to this planet, had been sent back punished and in disgrace after he'd kidnapped Elise and tried to take her for himself. She hadn't been his mate. That was the big difference between him and me. And I hadn't kidnapped her. I'd saved her from a creature that had been about to attack her and the other human. Yes, I could have brought her here, but I had witnessed my brother Cerban's struggle with the dating agency's fixed rules and regulations when he'd found his mate in Maelis. They had tried to keep them apart just because there hadn't been any evidence that they were mates. I'd personally had to smuggle Maelis into his room while he'd been under house arrest.

I didn't want that for myself. I'd rather break the rules and stay away from the island until... Until when? Until Verity had come to the realisation that we were mates? Until I'd somehow got a DNA sample off her to add to the Hot Tatties database, proving that there was a match between us?

I pulled myself from my thoughts. I shouldn't linger here for longer than necessary. My clutch-brothers were surely wondering already where I'd disappeared to. Hopefully, they assumed I'd gone on a long, solitary swim in the ocean and would return soon. Tomorrow, I'd be expected to work.

Cerban's hut was next. He and Maelis had been assigned the house after their relationship had become official. Its door stood open to the warm night, soft music drifting out from a small device Maelis treasured. They sat close together on the porch, heads touching, the glow of a lamp turning her hair to dark gold.

A wave of guilt hit me hard. My brothers had found peace here, and I was about to break the trust we'd built together.

I ducked into the shadows, keeping to the trees as I slipped past them. My old quarters were in the main accommodation block where all the single finmen were housed. I avoided the main door, where a few other males were lingering, and instead headed straight to my window. I was glad my room was on the ground floor. And as luck would have it, I hadn't closed the window properly. I pushed it open, then climbed into my room.

The room smelled faintly of salt and oil, the scent of home. My belongings were few — some clothes, a knife and other weapons, an old waterproof bag from my navy days. I stuffed it with what I needed: a blanket, a towel, a fire-starter, fruit from the bowl the local staff always refilled in the morning, a chocolate bar - I'd come to love that human treat - and a small metal cup. In the wardrobe, I found a human-sized shirt that I'd forgotten to give to the staff. At the last moment, I added a light waterproof cloak; it would drown her in fabric, but at least she'd be covered.

Footsteps crunched on the path outside. Voices followed. I froze. I'd lingered for too long.

"Still no sign of him?" That was Fionn. Calm but wary.

Cerban's reply came quieter, but edged with concern. "He's not on patrol. I checked the logs. He left hours ago."

"Maybe he's sulking again." That was Elise, teasing. "He does that when he's moody."

"I don't think so," Fionn said softly. "He seemed... restless today. If he's gone too far, the current might—"

"No." Cerban's voice was firm. "He knows these waters better than most of us." A pause. "But if he's not back by dawn, we'll send a drone. Or look for him with the *Tidebound*'s scanners."

The words sent a jolt through me. They couldn't find me. Not now. Not with her.

I scanned the room for paper and found a scrap torn from a shipping manifest, the back still blank. I hesitated, then wrote quickly in blocky human letters:

All is well. Do not search. Will return when ready.

It wasn't a lie, not really. I'd return — just not yet.

I left the note on the little desk, then I slung the bag over my shoulder and climbed back through the window, into the night.

The path to the sea ran quiet now. Voices had faded, replaced by the soft murmur of the tide. I paused once, looking back at the glowing huts, at the place that had been home. For the first time, it felt distant.

"Forgive me, brothers," I whispered. "You have your mates. Let me have mine."

The water closed around me, cool and clean. I kicked off from the sand and swam hard, the dark current carrying me toward the small islet where my future waited.

6

Verity

I t was dark when I woke, but the light of a fire flickered through the blackness. The smell of smoke mixed with the scent of salt and kelp coming from the dried seaweed still covering my naked body. And beneath the thick smoke was another smell, one that made my mouth water: freshly baked fish.

He was back, sitting with his back to me, stoking the fire. Shadows danced over his green skin, making him look even more alien.

Was that what he was? An alien? Or was he a merman from the legends come to life? My grandma had always said that all legends were rooted in reality. Maybe the stories of mermaids and sea folk had their basis in people like him.

But this was the twenty-first century. There were satellites, sonar, internet. I highly doubted mythical creatures could hide from view as easily now as they could have centuries ago.

"You're awake." He said it without turning around. "I have made fish. And I have brought you something warmer to wear. Are you cold?"

"Freezing."

He got up, stretching to his full length, towering above me. He was taller than I'd remembered. He pulled a simple t-shirt from a bag, followed by a bundle of fabric.

"I believe this is what you humans wear," he said, hesitation lacing his voice. "I am not sure if it is meant for males or females. And it will likely be too big for you..."

Was he really as insecure as he sounded in this moment? Or was this an act to lull me into a fall sense of security?

I took it from him. "It will do. Turn around."

The shirt was definitely a man's, falling down to my thighs, but I didn't mind. It felt a whole lot better than the kelp covering. Rainse wordlessly handed me the fabric. It turned out to be a sort of cloak, made from a shimmering, light fabric unlike anything I'd ever seen before. I was looking forward to further inspecting it in daylight. My mother had been a seamstress, and I'd grown up surrounded by cupboards, boxes, shelves full of fabric. My dad had always said that she had an addiction.

I wrapped the cloak around myself like a blanket. Despite the thin material, I immediately felt warmer. But even better, I no longer felt vulnerable and exposed. What a difference clothes could make.

He still had his back turned to me. The flames threw enough light for me to see the play of muscles beneath the green sheen of his skin. Strange, beautiful, otherworldly.

When I sat down again, the sand was warm against my legs, the fire crackling softly between us. He offered me a piece of fish, wrapped in a broad leaf that gleamed with oil. I hesitated only long enough to test the smell—fresh, salty, cooked perfectly—and then ate. It was delicious, far better than anything I'd expected to find on a deserted island.

I was ravenous. When I'd finished the fish, he wordlessly handed me another one.

"What about you?" I asked, still chewing.

"I have already eaten."

Now that my initial hunger was sated and I was less cold, I could think more clearly again. And something didn't quite add up for me.

"How did you get all this stuff?" I asked, trying to keep my voice level. I didn't want to turn this into an argument with a stranger on whom I was entirely reliant. Not yet, anyway. "Where did you get the shirt? The matches to make a fire? The bag next to you?"

He looked into the flames instead of at me. "From the island."

"The island," I echoed. "You mean *this* island?"

"No. The other one."

My pulse picked up. "So there's another island nearby?"

His jaw tightened, the faint green tendrils along his shoulders shifting. "Yes."

"Then why didn't you take me there?"

I pushed the words out too quickly, and a stab of pain caught me under the ribs. I winced, covering it with a breath that hurt almost as much. "You think I can't handle it?"

For the first time, he hesitated. His eyes flicked toward me, dark and unreadable. "The sea is not kind to the wounded. You would not survive the swim. "It is not safe for you."

"Wounded?" I shot back. "I'm fine."

"You make a sound when you inhale too deeply."

I let out a shaky breath just to spite him—and immediately regretted it as pain lanced across my side. He didn't move, but the tendrils along his shoulders twitched as though reacting to my discomfort.

"I'm fine," I muttered, mostly to myself. "It's just a bruise."

"Bruises fade," he said quietly. "But water does not forgive weakness. It is not safe."

"Not safe?" I laughed softly, the sound too brittle. "And here is? You've got to be kidding me. There's nothing on this rock but sand, kelp, and coconuts. And even those coconuts will all be gone soon."

"You would not understand," he said quietly.

"Try me."

"I am a finman. I was born underwater and I will die underwater. My body is made for it." He tapped the sides of his neck. "I have gills. I can breathe beneath the ocean's surface. I have webbing between my toes to increase my swim speed. I have greenskin that reads the currents and helps me plan my route. I can hear, see, smell better than humans, both underwater and on land. For me, swimming to the island was easy. I could navigate the dangerous currents. Sea creatures like the one that almost attacked you know I am a fiercer predator than they are. They won't dare to attack me."

"Well, you've just established that you're better than me," I sighed, frustrated at the lack of actual information. "But not why you didn't bring me to the island that has shirts and blankets and food. Or why you didn't bring me back to my ship, the *Minerva*. You didn't know I had a cracked, broken, whatever rib when you first rescued me."

He stared into the flames, not meeting my eyes. He was hiding something, I was sure of it.

"It would be too dangerous," he said eventually. "There are sea creatures near the island that are much more aggressive than the one you encountered. They would see you as prey, even with me by your side. And besides, the currents are too strong there just now. I could swim through them, but I couldn't drag you along."

I didn't believe a single word of it. Yes, there were sharks in these waters. He'd already proven that he could handle them. And currents? Seriously?

But I didn't want to alienate him. Not yet. I'd find a way to discover the real reason why he was keeping me here. And then I'd escape. For now, I'd let him think that I'd accepted his excuses.

"Who are you, really?" I asked abruptly. "A merman? An alien? Something else?"

He looked relieved at the change of topic. "I was born on the planet of Finfolkaheem, which makes me an alien in your eyes - even though it is you who is the alien, to me." He grinned. It lit up his face, making him seem younger and less stern.

"If you're an alien, then how come you understand me? How come you speak English?"

He tapped the side of his head. "I have a translator implant. But I have also spent some time learning your language. Without the implant, I'd be able to communicate, but I'd get lost in translation a lot, so for now, I'm relying on it. Your Earth languages are very different from the ones we speak on Finfolkaheem. Yours are made to carry through air. Ours are made to echo through water." He hesitated for a moment. "Would you like me to tell you about my world?"

I looked up at the moon, trying to judge what time it was. But then I decided it didn't matter. I wasn't tired. I'd eaten my fill of fish. And I wasn't going to get off this tiny island tonight. So I might as well listen to his stories.

For some reason, I didn't react with panic or shock at the revelation that he was an alien. I supposed a lot of strange things had happened since this morning. A whale had crashed into my boat. A shark had almost eaten me. And now I was listening to an alien tell me about his home. I rubbed my forehead. Maybe I'd cracked my head. Maybe I was dreaming. Maybe I was in a coma. Or maybe this was all real and I was just too stunned to react in a normal, scream-in-panic kind of way.

I nodded. "Please do."

He stared into the distance, and I imagined him picturing his home, remembering places I could only dream of.

"I grew up in the city of Eynhallow, brought up with two clutch-brothers called Fionn and Cerban. I am the oldest of us three, but by less than a sunpass. Still, as finboys, I would often make a point of being the oldest, and therefore in charge." He chuckled and once again I was struck at how a simple smile changed his entire appearance. "My planet is beautiful. Most finfolk live underwater, in large cities or small hamlets at the bottom of the ocean. Others prefer to travel as nomads, traversing the seas as traders and storytellers. Life as a finboy was good, until we reached adulthood. That's when... No, I need to explain some things first. Generations ago, the climate of Finfolkaheem began to change. The oceans grew warmer. And that affected the gender of the finbabes being born. Fewer and fewer females, more and more males."

"Like turtles."

"Turtles?" he asked, confused.

"They lay eggs in sand and the sand's temperature determines the gender. Although for them, it seems it's the opposite way than for your kind. Warmer sand means more females. But I suppose the end result is the same."

He nodded, sadness now creasing his brow. "We reached a point where for every ten males, only one female was born. That's when the Matriarchs created a new system that would ensure the survival of our species. All finboys were to be tested and only the best would be assigned a female."

I could see where this was going, but I stayed silent.

"My clutch-brothers and I were deemed unworthy. We were told that we would never have a mate. It was devastating."

The pain was etched into his face, shimmering in his dark eyes. I felt for him. I really did.

"I'm sorry," I said when he didn't continue.

Rainse stared into the flames. "It took me a long time to come to terms with. And I'm not sure if my clutch-brother Fionn ever did. He was miserable. In a way, it was fitting that it was him who discovered our one hope of finding mates."

"How?"

"He found a record in the National Archives that spoke of a group of finfolk who had crash-landed on a planet far away. They had stayed there for hundreds of mooncrossings - years in your language. Their presence would give rise to legends about sentient beings living in the sea, although for some reason, they ended up being depicted with fish tails instead of legs."

"Mermaids," I whispered. "They crashed on Earth."

"Yes, they did. Until recently, we thought they'd lived only near the country of Scotland, but my brother and his mate found evidence that they also lived here, in this area. And they had unions with the locals. With humans. And those unions resulted in children."

The wonder in his voice was evident. I wasn't quite sure what to think about it all, if I could believe this fairy tale, but to him, it meant hope.

"Eventually, the stranded finfolk were rescued," he continued. "And their story was forgotten. I don't know if it was through the passage of time or orchestrated on purpose, but for a long time, nobody knew about your planet and the potential it bears. Until Fionn found the records. An acquaintance of ours, Kelon, organised a ship. That is how we came to be here."

"And were you successful? In finding wives?"

I wasn't sure if I wanted to know the answer. I didn't want him to tell me that he was married with three adorable finman-human children. Even though that should have made me happy for him. I'd seen the pain on his face when he'd spoken of the moment he'd been told that he'd always be alone. It must have been awful. I was single out of choice, not because some higher authority had forbidden me to find a partner. That was something very different.

"My clutch-brothers have mates. Fionn was the first. He now lives with Elise, while Cerban and Maelis are absolutely besotted with each other."

"Are you jealous?" I blurted before I could stop myself. The edge in his voice had spoken of envy and sadness.

He turned to me, his face illuminated by the fire, his eyes glowing otherworldly.

"Yes, I am. I am ashamed to admit it, but it would not be honourable to lie about that. I wish with all my heart that I had what they have. It is the reason we came to this planet, after all. Just like all the other unmated males, my details have been added to a database. As soon as a match is found, I will be notified. But so far, there have been no news. I wait every sunpass. Every click. Until now... silence. But... No."

"What were you going to say?"

"It is getting late. You should get some sleep. It will help your recovery. We shall talk more tomorrow."

I was about to protest, but a yawn rose in my throat, belying the argument I'd already sketched out in my head. Maybe it would be better to wait until tomorrow. I needed my full strength to read between his lines and figure out what was really going on.

I stared at him across the flames, at the alienness in his features. What had he called the growths on his shoulders, arms and hips? Greenskin. I realised it wasn't skin at all but something alive, growing from him in long, thin fronds that caught every flicker of light. They reminded me of the kelp forests I'd studied during my honours degree—sensitive to motion, to water flow, to sound. They moved when the air changed, as though tasting it.

"Can you move them? Your greenskin?" I asked before I could stop myself.

He looked down at the nearest strand where it coiled against his ribs. "No. I don't have that sort of control over it. But it reacts, listens, senses. It tells me when the currents change, when danger swims close."

"Like a sensory organ." My scientific brain was already cataloguing possibilities, theories, comparisons to fish lateral lines.

"Yes," he said simply. "Exactly that."

Curiosity overrode caution. I reached out, my hand shaking only a little, and brushed my fingertips against one of the kelp fronds near his shoulder. It was soft and cool, supple as seaweed, pulsing faintly beneath my touch as if it recognised me.

Rainse went utterly still. "It listens to you too," he said, voice quiet and unreadable.

I snatched my hand back, half in alarm, half in wonder. "Sorry. I didn't mean—"

"You are curious. That is good." He turned back to the fire, feeding another stick into the flames. "Rest now. Tomorrow the sea may calm. Then we will see what the tide allows."

It wasn't a promise, but it wasn't a refusal either. My ribs throbbed with every breath, making argument impossible. I lay back on the sand, the warmth of the fire against my side, the sound of waves whispering around us.

I told myself I'd question everything properly in the morning. For now, I pulled the cloak tighter around my body and let the crackle of fire and the pulse of the ocean lull me toward uneasy sleep.

7

Rainse

She was still sleeping when I woke at the first light of dawn. Earth had the best sunrises. On Finfolkaheem, they were milky and washed out, while here the colours were bright and beautiful. I sat in the sand next to the burned out fire and watched the sun rise while listening to the soft sound of Verity's breathing.

She stirred in her sleep, a soft sigh escaping her lips. The sound went through me like a current. My greenskin twitched along my shoulders and ribs, reading the rhythm of her breath, mapping it against the pulse of the sea. The bond hummed quietly, a reminder that she was mine, even if she didn't know it yet.

I told myself it was enough just to watch her. To make sure she was safe. To breathe in a world where she existed.

When I couldn't stand the stillness any longer, I rose and walked down to the water. The surf curled around my feet, warm from the sun. Small silver fish darted through the shallows, unbothered by my presence. I caught two in quick succession and laid them on a flat rock to clean later.

Every movement felt purposeful. Controlled. Because if I stopped moving, I'd start thinking—about the brothers I'd left behind, the lies I'd built, the future that could crumble with one human word.

I gathered driftwood and kindling, coaxing a new flame from the embers of the night's fire. By the time the first crackle filled the silence, she was awake.

"You're up early," she murmured, her voice rough with sleep. She pushed herself up on one elbow, blinking against the light. The borrowed shirt hung loose on her frame, one shoulder bare. My throat went tight.

"The sea doesn't sleep," I said, crouching to tend the fire. "And neither do I, for long."

She smiled faintly. "You sound like a proverb."

"Finfolk sayings," I admitted. "My people like to make everything sound wise."

"And are they?" she asked.

"Sometimes." I glanced at her ribs, noting the way she winced as she straightened. "You should rest. The bruising hasn't faded."

"It's fine," she said, brushing it off, though her breath hitched slightly. "I need to move around. My muscles are stiff."

I stood and offered her my hand. She hesitated before taking it, her fingers small and warm against mine. The contact sent another pulse through the bond, sharp enough to make me release her too soon.

"Sorry," she said quickly, misreading my reaction. "Did I—hurt you?"

"No." My voice came out lower than intended. "You could never hurt me."

Her gaze flicked up, curious but cautious. "That's a dangerous thing to say."

"Only if it's a lie."

Silence stretched between us, filled with the steady sigh of the waves. I turned back to the fire before I said something even more foolish.

"I'll make breakfast," I said. "Stay here. The sand's softest by the rocks."

She nodded, still watching me as I waded into the water again. The sea was cool and welcoming. If I hadn't been hungry, I would have liked to go for a long dive. My greenskin brushed against the current, tasting it. Something about the pattern felt strange—an odd static under the surface, too erratic to be wind or an oncoming storm.

A warning.

The sea was changing.

I looked back once. Verity had her face tilted toward the sun, eyes closed, trusting me completely. The bond thrummed louder, possessive and fierce.

"Don't stray too far," I whispered to the wind. "Not today."

I caught a few more fish, eating one raw in the water so she wouldn't see just how different I was from her. I could eat cooked fish, of course, but it would never taste as good as freshly caught and raw.

By the time the fish were cooked, the smell had drawn her closer to the fire. She moved carefully, still favouring her ribs, one hand pressed against her side.

"Smells good," she said, settling cross-legged in the sand. "I didn't know you could cook."

"It isn't cooking," I replied. "Just heating."

"Still counts." She smiled faintly, and for a heartbeat, the world stopped turning. Her smile wasn't bright or careless like my brothers' mates'. It was small and quiet, like sunlight through deep water.

I handed her a piece of fish wrapped in a broad leaf. She accepted it, sniffed, then took a bite. "Salty," she said through a mouthful. "But in a good way."

"Salt is life." I sat opposite her, the fire between us. "We are made of the same sea."

"That's poetic," she said, chewing thoughtfully. "Do all your people talk like that?"

"Only when we forget how to be practical."

She laughed softly, and something warm bloomed in my chest. I hadn't realised how much I missed laughter.

"So," she said after a moment, "what do Finfolk do when they're not saving stranded humans or making over-salted fish?"

"We swim. We work. We fight. Sometimes we sing."

"Sing?"

"Not with words. With resonance." I gestured to the faint green tendrils that curled along my ribs. "The greenskin carries sound through water. When enough of us sing together, the ocean vibrates."

She looked fascinated. "That's... beautiful. Like whale song."

"Whales borrowed it from us," I said, only half teasing.

"Of course they did," she said dryly, but her lips curved. "I study them, you know. Marine mammals.

Mostly orcas, but I've worked with minkes too. I was in the field for data collection when the accident happened."

"The accident." The word felt too small for what had nearly taken her from me.

"Our boat got hit. By a whale." She paused, her voice quieter now. "A humpback. I saw its fluke just before it struck. It shouldn't have behaved like that — they're not aggressive. We weren't even close enough to startle it."

I stayed silent. I was unsure what exactly a whale was, but I could imagine it was one of the great, gentle creatures that sometimes sang to us across the depths. They were not violent by nature. But the oceans of this planet held more secrets than the humans realised.

"It felt deliberate," she added softly. "Like it wanted us gone."

"Maybe it did," I said. "The sea has its own rules."

"Yeah," she said, giving a tired smile. "I'm starting to learn that."

"Why were you on that boat in the first place? I have found humans will stay on land for most of their lives."

"Not all humans. I am a marine biologist. I study life in the oceans. It would be hard to do that without going out, collecting samples, observing nature, discovering the genius solutions nature has developed to problems we don't even know about yet. I go on at least one big expedition each year. This one was supposed to last two months. But now... You said Jammie... James is safe. But what about Hugo? Did you see a third person in the water when you found the two of us?"

I tried to think back to that moment I'd first sensed them from far away. "I don't believe I did. Maybe he had already been rescued by the time I got there?"

She seemed so tense that I wanted to reach out and draw her close. But I resisted the urge. She wasn't ready. Not yet.

"I hope so," she muttered. "It's strange. Twenty-four hours ago, I was climbing into the RIB to look for whales. Now I'm sitting on a beach in borrowed clothes, eating alien fish."

"Alien fish?"

"You caught it. You cooked it. That makes it alien by association."

I smiled before I could stop myself. "Then you are alien now too. You have eaten alien fish."

"Oh no," she said, mock horror in her voice. "Is that how it works? Some kind of ritual?"

"Perhaps," I said lightly. "Too late to undo it now."

Her laughter broke the tension that had been coiling between us since dawn. I wanted to hold on to that sound, keep it safe.

"You're not what I expected," she said after a pause. "You're quieter. Kinder. I thought..."

"You thought monsters from the deep would have sharper teeth?"

"Something like that," she admitted. "But you don't seem like someone who enjoys scaring people."

"I used to," I said honestly. "When I was younger. Before I learned what fear does to the world."

She studied me for a moment, her eyes thoughtful. "You've seen a lot, haven't you?"

"Enough to know that peace is rare. And fragile."

Her expression softened. "You sound like someone who's lost it before."

"Many times." I looked out at the sea. "But perhaps it is returning."

She didn't answer, but her gaze lingered on me a little longer than before. The morning light made her eyes the colour of shallow water—green, gold, alive. I had to look away first.

The bond hummed quietly beneath my skin, patient but insistent. I wondered if she could feel it too, that slow, tidal pull drawing us closer with every breath.

When she'd finished her fish, she got to her feet. She repressed a groan of pain, but it was too late, I had heard it.

"You should rest," I said gently.

"I have rested enough. I want to see what kind of island I am stranded on."

I jumped to my feet. "Let me give you the grand tour."

She arched an eyebrow. "Grand, huh? I've seen bigger sandbanks."

"You haven't seen *this* one." I swept an arm toward the copse of trees, trying not to smile. "Behold—the most popular attraction of the island: the famous coconut tree."

She followed me, limping only a little, her hand pressed to her side. "Wow," she said gravely. "Such majesty. Truly the eighth wonder of the world."

"Visitors come from all corners of the ocean to admire it," I said. "It's rumoured to have survived at least five storms and three very persistent crabs."

That earned a laugh. The sound filled the quiet like birdsong, bright and unexpected. I wanted her to laugh again, and again, until I got used to the sound - although deep inside I knew that I would never get used to it, always appreciate it.

"And over here," I continued, pointing to a scatter of tide pools between the rocks, "we have our state-of-the-art aquarium. Entry is free. Please don't touch the residents—they bite."

She crouched to peer into one of the pools. A small crab scuttled sideways, unimpressed. "So no souvenir shells?"

"Only if you can outwit the locals," I said. "They guard their treasures fiercely."

"Where is the gift shop?"

"Currently closed for renovations. As is the on-site restaurant."

She glanced over her shoulder, grinning. "Do you ever give normal tours, or is this a Finfolk thing?"

"Normal is overrated." I stopped beside the darker rocks on the far side of the island. "And here we have the prestigious Cliff of Contemplation. Perfect for brooding or dramatic monologues."

"You're surprisingly funny for someone who barely smiles," she said, studying me.

"I smile when it's worth it."

"Am I worth it?"

The question hit harder than she meant it to. I managed a faint smile. "You are the first guest to appreciate my humour. That counts for something."

"High praise." She eased herself down on a smooth rock and looked out at the endless water. "You know, for a place this small, it's not half bad."

"It has everything you need," I said quietly. "Food. Shelter. Safety."

"And company," she added.

The words settled between us like the hush after a wave breaks. My greenskin rippled, sensing the shift in the air. For once, I didn't try to hide it.

"Yes," I said softly. "And company."

She smiled, turning her face toward the wind. "So, what do you call this paradise?"

"I haven't named it."

"You should," she said. "If you live somewhere long enough, it deserves a name."

"Then you name it," I said.

She thought for a moment, the corners of her mouth twitching. "How about... Coconutopia?"

I blinked. "That sounds like a disease."

She laughed again—louder this time—and I decided I could live with that sound for the rest of my life.

"All right then," she said once her laughter subsided. "You pick a name."

"Me?" I pretended to think deeply. "How about... Shell Island?"

"Too obvious."

"Fish Rock?"

"Uninspired."

"Storm Refuge?"

"Dramatic."

I rubbed my chin. "Kelp Haven?"

She gave me a flat look. "You just named it after your body."

"It's a feature, not a theme," I protested.

She snorted. "You really need to work on your marketing."

"Fine." I pointed toward the sea, where the sunlight scattered in shards across the surface. "Sunwater Isle."

Her expression softened. "That's... actually beautiful."

"You approve?"

"I do." She looked out over the water again, smiling faintly. "It fits. It feels like a pause between worlds. Somewhere that isn't quite one thing or the other."

"A pause," I echoed. "Yes. That's what this place is."

She tilted her head. "Do you have a word for that? In your language?"

I hesitated. "There's a Finfolk term—*vairu'ath*. It means a quiet space between currents."

"*Vairu'ath*," she repeated slowly, shaping the sounds carefully. "I like that better than Coconutopia."

"So do I."

The sea breeze lifted her hair, scattering a few strands across her face. She brushed them away absently, still gazing at the horizon. "Well then, *vairu'ath* it is. Our island."

"Our island," I murmured. The bond pulsed quietly in agreement, a heartbeat beneath my skin. I felt it echo in the water, carrying her name out into the waves. For the first time since I'd left my brothers, the ocean around me felt like home.

8

Verity

I looked up at the coconut tree, wondering how on Earth we were going to get those fruit down. One had fallen down, waiting to be opened, but we couldn't wait for them all to slowly drop to the ground. I wasn't much of a climber, and Rainse's webbed feet were not made for it either. Maybe we could shake the tree, together. Or we could-

What was I doing? For a moment, I'd forgotten that this wasn't real. That I was trapped on this island with him, an alien, who'd chosen not to bring me to the island where his brothers were, but instead chosen to isolate us on this islet.

I wasn't supposed to be thinking about coconuts and teamwork. I was supposed to be finding a way off this rock, not wondering how to make a tropical breakfast with my captor.

Captor. The word felt wrong every time I tried it on. He didn't act like one. He didn't lock me up or threaten me. He just... existed beside me. Quiet, watchful, frustratingly calm.

Rainse was crouched at the water's edge, cleaning something in the shallows. The sun caught the wet gleam of his greenskin, turning the fronds along his ribs and arms translucent. I told myself I was studying him the way I'd study a new marine species —curious, detached, professional. My pulse didn't get the memo.

He glanced back over his shoulder, eyes catching the light like sea glass. "You should stay in the shade. The sun is strong today."

"I'm fine," I said automatically. "I'm British. We only burn on holidays."

He frowned slightly, probably translating that through whatever alien logic filter he had. "If you burn, I will find waterweed to cool it."

"That's... considerate," I said, and then hated how uncertain it sounded.

He stood, tall and graceful, the movement too fluid to be entirely human. "You are healing. You move easier today."

"Barely," I muttered, rubbing at my ribs. "It still feels like I lost a fight with a steel beam."

"That is what the ocean is," he said. "A thousand steel beams, moving very fast."

I smiled despite myself. "I'll have to remember that for my next research paper."

His head tilted slightly, a habit of his when he didn't quite follow the joke but wanted to. "You will write again?"

The question hit harder than expected. I looked away, out toward the endless water. "If I get off this island, sure."

"You will," he said simply, as if it were a fact of physics.

I wanted to believe him. The problem was, I also wanted to punch him for sounding so certain.

"Maybe we should focus on coconuts first," I said, stepping closer to the tree. "Priorities."

He followed, watching with mild curiosity as I studied the trunk. "They are heavy," he said. "If one falls, it could crush you."

"Great pep talk, thanks." I glanced up at the cluster of fruit swaying against the bright sky. "If I die, at least it'll be ironic. Death by coconut, the marine biologist who survived both a whale and a shark attack."

"You will not die."

"You can't guarantee that."

"I can," he said, calm as ever. "Because I will not let it happen."

I stared at him, half irritated, half... something else. "You really don't do half measures, do you?"

"Half measures sink ships," he said, and that made me laugh.

The sound startled a flock of small seabirds from the rocks. They wheeled above us, shrieking against the bright blue, and for a heartbeat, everything felt almost normal.

But normal didn't last long out here. The wind brought a hint of something sour and briny, the kind of smell that meant too many tiny lives drifting close together. Rainse's expression changed, eyes narrowing as his greenskin rippled with movement.

"Stay here," he said, already striding toward the shore.

I watched him go, the strange tendrils along his body flaring like warning flags, and a cold prickle of unease ran down my spine. Whatever was in the water, it wasn't just fish.

"What are you doing?" I asked when he entered the water.

"I want to know what's going on. Something is different. I want to make sure you're safe."

I swept my arms in a wide circle, then winced at the sharp pain in my ribs. "I'm on an island. Not in the water. I'm safe. So are you. Why risk going for a swim when there is no need?"

He turned toward me, the water swirling around his legs. "Because the sea doesn't change without reason. I can feel it."

"Feel it?" I crossed my arms, immediately regretting the movement when my ribs protested. "What does that even mean?"

He hesitated, searching for words. "The currents. The charge beneath the surface. Something is wrong."

I frowned. The scientist in me wanted to challenge him —currents didn't have emotions, they had patterns. But the fronds along his shoulders were shifting restlessly, catching the light like living ribbons. They responded to things I couldn't sense, and that unsettled me more than I wanted to admit.

"You can't fix the ocean," I said, trying for humour. "Maybe it's just having a mood swing."

His lips curved faintly. "If the sea has moods, then this one feels angry."

That sent a small chill down my spine. "Then come back out."

"I will," he promised, eyes scanning the water. "Once I know why it's angry."

I sighed, half annoyed, half impressed by his persistence. "Fine. Just—don't get eaten or caught in a net or electrocuted or whatever it is that happens to Finfolk who ignore common sense."

He looked back over his shoulder, that faint, maddening smile still in place. "We don't get electrocuted. Usually."

"That's comforting."

He took another step deeper, until the water reached his waist, greenskin shifting like kelp caught in a tide. "Stay on the shore," he said quietly. "If anything happens, go to the rocks."

"You're assuming I'll listen."

"You won't," he said, not unkindly. "But I had to try."

He waded deeper until the water reached his chest, then dove elegantly beneath the surface. For a few seconds, I could still see him—just the faint shimmer of his greenskin gliding through the clear water. Then he was gone.

The sea looked harmless enough from here. Calm, even. Gentle waves lapped at the sand, innocent as anything, sparkling in the light of the sun. But every time I'd thought the ocean was harmless, it had proved me wrong.

I sat down on a flat rock, wrapping my arms around my knees. He'd said he'd be back soon. He'd also said he wouldn't get electrocuted, and I wasn't entirely sure I trusted either statement.

The minutes dragged. I watched the water, scanning for any sign of him. Every flicker of light beneath the surface could have been him—or just sunlight bouncing off sand.

What if he didn't come back?

The thought settled in my gut like a stone. If something happened to him, I'd be alone here. Completely alone. No rescue, no idea which direction to swim even if I could. My ribs ached just from breathing too deeply; I wouldn't make it halfway to anywhere.

I should have felt angry at him for leaving me like this, diving headfirst into danger because the water *felt different*. But anger didn't sit right. Not when I kept replaying the way he'd said *I want to make sure you're safe* as if it mattered more than his own life.

Maybe that's why I couldn't stop watching the water, waiting for that flash of green. I told myself it was practical—if he drowned, I'd needed to know—but that sounded hollow even inside my head.

I tried to think like a scientist. If he was injured, maybe he'd drift toward the shallows. Maybe the current would bring him back here. Maybe—

"Stop it," I muttered. "He's fine."

The ocean didn't care what I thought. It just kept breathing, slow and endless, like something alive.

The light changed, the sun dipping higher. Still no sign of him. My heart thudded painfully against my ribs, a dull echo of the pulse that had become too familiar—the one I sometimes felt in my chest when he looked at me for too long.

I pressed a hand to my sternum, as if I could quiet it. "You're not connected," I told myself. "You're just losing it."

A shadow moved beneath the water, far out by the darker reefs. Too large, too fast. I rose instinctively, scanning the waves.

"Rainse?" I called, then cursed myself for doing it. My voice carried out across the stillness and vanished into the blue.

The waves whispered back in a language I didn't speak. Every few seconds, the surface of a patch of water maybe twenty metres from the shore flickered — tiny bursts of light like lightning trapped under glass. Bioluminescence. I'd seen it before, just never this bright.

Then the light pulsed again, stronger. And another. The whole patch of water shimmered like a living constellation.

"Rainse?"

No answer. But something was wrong with the pattern. The glow wasn't rhythmic or steady — it flared in short, violent bursts. I'd seen that once, on a research trip to Fiji, when a jellyfish bloom got tangled in a propeller. They flashed like that when disturbed or attacked.

I walked into the shallows, shielding my eyes from the sun. The glow in front of me brightened, then fractured. For a heartbeat, I thought it was just reflection — until I saw him. His body twisted beneath the surface, the greenskin along his ribs thrashing with frantic light. Around him, jellyfish. So many of them.

"Rainse!"

My feet moved before my brain caught up. I took three steps into deeper water before logic slammed into me like a physical force.

Stop. Think.

Diving straight into that swarm would be suicide. I'd be stung within seconds, paralyzed, drowning beside him. And then we'd both be dead.

My hands were shaking. My ribs throbbed with every panicked breath.

Think like a scientist. Observe. Assess. Act.

The jellyfish were concentrated around him, drawn to something—the electrical pulses of his greenskin, maybe, or the thrashing of his body. They pulsed with each movement, releasing more venom with each contact.

I needed to disperse them. Get them away from him before I could pull him out.

I turned and ran.

My feet slipped on wet sand, my injured ribs screaming in protest, but I didn't stop. Driftwood. I needed something long, something to keep distance between me and those translucent bells of death.

There—a thick branch, sun-bleached and solid, half-buried in sand near the tree line. I yanked it free, testing its weight. Heavy, but I could manage. Long enough.

When I splashed back into the water, my heart was hammering so hard I could feel it in my throat.

What if I'm too late?

No. Not an option.

The jellyfish had drifted closer to shore, still clustered around that spot where I'd last seen him. I waded in up to my thighs, then my waist, forcing myself to move slowly despite every instinct screaming at me to rush.

The first jellyfish brushed my leg.

Fire. Pure, searing fire spreading across my calf.

I bit down on a scream and kept moving.

Using the branch, I swept through the water in wide arcs, pushing the jellyfish away from the centre of the swarm. They drifted, their bells pulsing indignantly, but they moved. The bioluminescence scattered, breaking apart into individual sparks of light.

Another sting on my arm. Then my hip.

Keep going. Keep moving.

I could see him now—really see him. He floated face-down, motionless, his greenskin still spasming with erratic light. Too many stings. His body wasn't responding anymore.

"Come on, Rainse. Stay with me."

I swept the branch one more time, clearing a path, then dropped it and lunged forward.

His body was heavier than I expected—all that dense muscle, that alien physiology. I hooked my arm under his chest and kicked hard, pulling us both toward shore. My ribs shrieked. My stung leg barely responded.

A jellyfish brushed my shoulder. Another burst of fire, spreading down my back.

Ignore it. Move.

The current fought me, trying to drag us back out. My vision blurred at the edges—pain or exhaustion or both. I couldn't tell anymore.

"Not today," I hissed through clenched teeth. "You don't get to die on me, seaweed man."

My feet found sand. Solid ground. I hauled him the last few meters, half-dragging, half-carrying, until we were clear of the waterline. Then my legs gave out and we both collapsed onto the beach.

For a moment, I just lay there, gasping, my whole body on fire.

Then training kicked in.

Airway. Breathing. Circulation.

I rolled him onto his back. His chest was rising and falling—shallow, too shallow, but breathing. His greenskin was covered in angry welts, the fronds hanging limp and discoloured where the venom had done its work.

Stingers. I needed to get the stingers off.

My hands were shaking so badly I could barely control them. I grabbed a shell from the sand—smooth, flat—and began scraping along his skin, careful not to press too hard. The nearly-invisible filaments came away in sticky strands.

"Sorry," I muttered, even though he couldn't hear me. "Sorry, sorry, I know this hurts."

His greenskin twitched under my touch, still trying to respond even in this state.

There—the worst cluster, across his ribs where the greenskin was thickest. I worked methodically, scraping, checking, scraping again. My vision kept trying to blur. My own stings burned like brands.

Focus. He needs you to focus.

When I'd cleared all the visible stingers, I sat back on my heels and looked at my limited resources. No vinegar. No ice. No medical kit.

But there was coconut water.

I crawled to where the fallen coconut still lay, cracked it open with a rock—took three tries, my hands were shaking so badly—and poured the liquid over the worst of his welts.

It hissed faintly where it touched, steam rising for just an instant. Not vinegar, but it was acidic enough to help neutralise the venom. I hoped.

Using another shell, I scooped out the coconut meat and pressed it against the angry red marks on his chest, his arms, his neck. Cool. Soothing. Something.

Please work. Please let this work.

His heartbeat was rapid under my palm when I checked—too rapid, or maybe that was normal for finfolk, I had no way to know. His skin was too warm. Or too cold. I couldn't tell through my own fever-haze of pain.

I needed to monitor him. Keep watch. Make sure he kept breathing.

But my own body was starting to rebel. The stings on my legs and arms throbbed in time with my heartbeat. My vision kept swimming. The adrenaline that had carried me this far was draining away, leaving only exhaustion and pain.

Just for a minute. I'll just rest for one minute.

I lay down beside him, keeping one hand on his chest so I could feel if his breathing changed. The sand was warm. The sun was warm. Everything was warm except the cold knot of fear in my stomach.

"You're not dying," I told him firmly. "I didn't drag your heavy alien ass out of the ocean just to watch you die on this beach. So you're going to keep breathing, and you're going to wake up, and you're going to owe me. Again."

His greenskin pulsed once under my hand—so faint I almost missed it.

"That's right," I whispered. "You keep fighting."

The world tilted. My eyes drifted closed.

When I forced them open again, the sun had moved. An hour? Two? I couldn't tell.

But Rainse was still breathing. Slower now. Steadier.

I checked the coconut poultices—they'd dried out, crusted to his skin. But underneath, the welts looked better. Less angry. The greenskin had stopped its erratic pulsing.

Relief hit me so hard I started crying.

Stupid. Unprofessional. But I couldn't stop.

I'd saved him. The alien who'd saved me. We were even now.

Except it didn't feel even. It felt like something else entirely—something I wasn't ready to name.

I rested my forehead against his shoulder and let myself shake apart, just for a moment. Then I pulled myself together, checked his vitals again, and settled in to wait for him to wake up.

"You're going to owe me so much fish," I told him. "And an explanation for why you thought swimming into a jellyfish swarm was a good idea. And possibly a foot rub, because my legs are never going to forgive me for this."

His greenskin flickered—just once—and I chose to believe he'd heard me.

His skin felt warm under my hands. Too warm. I put a hand on his chest, hoping that he had a heart - and in the same place as mine. It was thumping rapidly. Was that normal for a finman or not? There was no way to know.

"You're not dying on me," I said firmly. "Not after I just saved you. I need you to wake up so we can celebrate that I returned the favour. I'm no damsel in distress. I'm a heroine."

Still no answer. I swallowed hard and leaned down until I could feel his breath against my cheek — shallow, but regular.

"Good," I whispered. "Stay that way."

A cold shiver ran over my back, and I realised that I was still wearing the wet oversized T-shirt. Where had Rainse put the clothes I'd worn when he'd fished me from the sea? I found them laid out to dry on a large flat rock. They were hard with salt, but they would do. This had to be the first time in all my life that I was glad to put on a bra. It gave me safety. Protection. Having my own clothes back felt good.

I sat next to Rainse, staring out onto the ocean, hoping for... What? A sign? One of his brothers?

If Rainse died, I wouldn't last long by myself. This tiny island wouldn't sustain me for long. But... that wasn't the only reason I didn't want him to die. I rested my hand on his chest again and closed my eyes, focusing on his heartbeat vibrating against my skin.

I didn't want him to die because...

No. I wouldn't even think it.

9

Rainse

The water was black in every direction, heavy and endless. I floated in the dark, listening for a current that wasn't there. No sound. No song. Just silence.

Then came the voices — the Matriarchs, cold and certain. "You are not chosen." Their words had always sounded like judgement wrapped in ritual. "You have fought too fiercely. Argued too often. The sea remembers anger."

I tried to speak, to beg, but the words tangled in the water. I reached for my brothers, but they were already fading into the distance, swimming toward light while I sank deeper into black.

The silence pressed against me until it became pain. *You are unworthy.*

The words echoed until they dissolved into something softer — a hum, a rhythm. The dark water warmed, light spreading from somewhere close. The silence became breath.

When I opened my eyes, I was no longer in Finfolkaheem. I was on the islet. The sun was low, gold spilling over the sea like molten glass. She was there, sitting on the shore with her knees drawn to her chest, hair tangled by wind, eyes bright against the light. She turned toward me and smiled — a small, real smile, one that reached all the way to her eyes.

"You're awake, my love," she said.

I blinked. The sea and the dream blurred together. The line between what had been and what could be vanished like foam.

"You're awake," she repeated — and this time her voice wasn't in the dream. It was beside me.

I turned my head. Reality crashed back. The sky above was soft with early morning light. The air smelled of salt, smoke, and her. She was lying next to me beneath the same cloak-turned-blanket, propped up on one elbow. She'd put her own clothes back on. Her hair brushed my shoulder.

Slowly, the memory returned. Darkness. Pain. A voice in the distance.

She'd saved me.

I remembered the flashes of light, the stinging sensation all over my body, the taste of pain like iron in my throat. And then her voice, calling through the water. Strong. Hopeful. Human.

I shifted carefully, sitting up slowly. For some reason, dried pieces of coconut were scattered across my chest, sticking to my skin and peeling off in places.

"You're alive," she said, squinting. "Good. That would've been a waste of effort."

My throat tightened around a laugh. "You saved me."

"You make it sound like you didn't give me a choice." She sat up, rubbing her eyes. "You really need to stop throwing yourself at everything that glows."

"I didn't know they would attack."

"You *felt* it, didn't you?" she asked. "That's what you said — the sea felt wrong. Did you think you were invincible? Sometimes, even the smallest things can be deadly. The ocean is not a safe place. And it is full of mysteries. I'm the first to admit that, despite all the science."

"How long was I asleep?"

"Since lunchtime yesterday. I kept a watch over you overnight, but I must have fallen asleep at some point. I was monitoring your breathing and heartbeat - not that I know what's normal for a finman. But they slowed down over time, so I took that as a good sign. And since I didn't have vinegar on hand, I had to resort to coconut." Her gaze wandered to my chest. "Looks like it worked. The burns are much better than they were yesterday."

"Thank you," I said quietly. "For saving my life."

She shrugged, but her cheeks coloured slightly. "You'd have done the same."

"I already did," I said before I could stop myself.

Her eyes twinkled. "Right. So we're even now."

I wanted to tell her that we'd always been even, that we were mates, but I bit down on the words. She wasn't ready for that truth yet.

"You should rest," I said instead. "You've done enough for one lifetime. I will make us some food soon. There are fish in the shallows. I won't need to go for a dive to find us a meal."

"You're not the boss of me," she said, lying back down anyway.

I smiled, unable to help it. "No," I murmured. "But I'd like to be the reason you never need saving again."

She was already drifting back to sleep, and I wasn't sure she'd heard me. Maybe that was for the best.

I lay beside her, listening to the waves. For the first time in years, the word *unworthy* felt far away, swallowed by the sea.

Something warm and soft was pressed against my chest. I breathed in deep and the realisation swept across me like an unexpected embrace. It was her. Verity. I must have fallen asleep, and she must have rolled against me - or maybe purposely snuggled against me.

I didn't dare move. Didn't want to breathe. The steady rhythm of her heartbeat against my ribs, slow and sure. Each pulse sent a tremor through the bond that hummed beneath my skin. It wasn't just a whisper anymore; it crackled with energy, alive and curious.

Every finman's bond with his mate was slightly different. Neither of my clutch-brothers had described it to feel this *electric*, but then, I hadn't asked them too many questions. I'd been too jealous and hadn't wanted to dwell on the sad fact that they had mates and I didn't.

She stirred and let out a soft, sleepy sound that did terrible things to my self-control. My body wanted to draw her closer, to surround her, to breathe her in until there was no line between us. My mind screamed to stay still. Humans didn't understand bonds. Not yet. Not until it was explained, chosen.

"Morning," she murmured, voice rough with sleep.

"Morning," I managed, the word a low rumble in my chest.

She blinked up at me, confused for a heartbeat before realising how close we were. Colour rose in her cheeks. She pushed herself upright, brushing hair from her face. "Sorry, I didn't—"

"Don't apologise," I said quickly. "You kept me warm."

That earned a half-smile. "Guess we're even then."

I almost said *not even close*. The bond thrummed again, a soft ache in my chest that made me glance toward the sea — and freeze.

The water beyond the reef was shifting, a column of bubbles rising in the distance. The current carried a sound I knew too well: the deep, rhythmic pulse of Finfolk resonance. A song of search and recognition.

Fionn. He'd found me.

I was on my feet before I'd even thought about it.

"What is it?" Verity asked, alarmed.

"My brother," I said. "He's coming."

"Here?"

I nodded. The water exploded as a tall figure broke the surface — green skin glinting in the sunlight, hair slicked back, eyes sharp and searching.

Verity gasped softly. "There are more of you."

"I told you," I said quietly. "I have brothers."

Fionn raised his hand in greeting. His expression didn't hold anger, just worry and relief. His gaze flicked to Verity. I instinctively blocked his view. He raised an eyebrow at that.

I cringed. Fionn was my brother. I should let him help me with this situation, not hide the truth from him.

"So that is why you've disappeared," Fionn sighed. Water pearled down his skin, and I imagined what he would look like to Verity - alien, masculine, attractive.

I had to stop being so jealous and protective. But it was hard to shut down those thoughts.

"Won't you introduce us?" Verity asked, stepping out of my shadow.

I'd known it wouldn't last. Taking my mate to this tiny island had been a desperate attempt for us to have privacy as we got to know each other. Avoid them taking her away from me. But it hadn't been long enough. I hadn't had the chance to tell her that she was my mate. It was all too soon.

I sighed. "Verity, this is Fionn, my clutch-brother and the interim leader of the finfolk on Earth. Fionn, this is Verity, an ocean scientist who I saved from the waves' clutch - and then she saved me."

Fionn nodded knowingly. "Yesterday. There was a disturbance in the water. It is why I went to search for you, to make sure you were safe. What happened?"

"I was attacked by huge, toothy monsters. They almost killed me."

Verity snort-laughed. "It was tiny jellyfish. No teeth or monsters involved." Her smile weakened. "But you are right. They did almost kill you. I don't know why they were attracted to you in such numbers, and why you reacted so strongly to their stings, but you would have drowned if I hadn't pulled you ashore."

"I would not. Finfolk can't drown."

Fionn sighed. "They can if they stop breathing for some reason. If what you say is true, Verity, you have my thanks for saving my brother's life. We are in your debt."

She looked at him as if she wasn't sure if he was serious. Then, she gracefully inclined her head. "It was a debt I owed. Now Rainse and I are even."

Fionn smiled. "It seems my brother has found his match. Have you talked about-"

"Not now," I interrupted.

"If it is obvious to me, it will be obvious to the other finmen on the island. And you can't stay here forever." He looked around the islet. "You haven't even got a shelter. A storm is approaching, you must have felt it. It may hit tomorrow, or the sunpass after, but it is coming. You are not safe to stay here."

"Verity is injured," I snapped. "I didn't want to risk the swim until she was better."

"Injured?" my clutch-brother asked sharply. "Then you should have contacted me immediately. We could have got her to a med pod."

Verity stepped forward. "It's just a cracked rib, nothing to worry about. But if you have a way for me off this island, I would be very grateful." She shot a dark look at me. "It seems Rainse forgot to mention that there are other routes to safety that don't involve swimming through dangerous currents and shark-infested waters."

I knew Fionn well enough to know that he was struggling with his self-control. He knew I'd kept the truth from Verity. And he didn't support that decision.

"Give me a moment to explain everything, brother. I thought... I thought I'd have more time."

His gaze softened. "I will go for a swim. I saw an interesting swarm of fish nearby that I want to take a closer look at. And Rainse... Make sure you tell her *everything*."

I swallowed hard as I watched him wade back into the water. I wasn't ready. Verity wasn't ready to hear the truth yet. If I told her now that she was my mate, she'd run. She didn't feel the bond the same way I did - none of the humans ever did. And once we got back to the island, they'd separate us until our mate bond had been verified by science. For that, Verity would have to consent to give a DNA sample. Would she even want to do that? And if she did, it would take several sunpasses for the results to come back. I couldn't be parted from her for that long. I just couldn't.

"Everything," Verity said sternly, her arms crossed in front of her chest. "Spill the beans."

"Beans?"

"It's an expression. It means, tell me everything. Now."

I sighed. "I will. Under one condition."

"I don't think you're in any state to make demands. Not after what your brother implied. But... I'll hear it."

"Promise me you will listen. Don't get up, don't run away, don't ask Fionn to take you to the other island until I've finished. Please."

She cocked her head to the side as she considered my words. Then, after a small eternity, she nodded.

"I will listen."

10

I wasn't sure what I'd expected when I told him to "spill the beans." Probably some explanation about alien culture or why he'd dragged me to this particular sandbank. I hadn't expected him to look as if he'd rather face a hurricane than talk to me.

Rainse sat opposite me, elbows on his knees, hands clasped so tightly his knuckles had gone pale green. For once, he didn't try to meet my eyes. The only sound between us was the low hush of waves licking at the shore.

"You said you'd listen," he began quietly.

"I am."

He nodded once, as if steadying himself. "Among my people, when two lives are... meant to be entwined, the sea recognises it. We call it the *bond*. It isn't magic. It's biology, or maybe chemistry. I'm not a scientist like you. It tells us when we've found the person we're meant to be with. To protect. To love."

Love. The word settled somewhere deep inside my heart.

"So, you're saying this is predetermined?" I asked. "Like some kind of built-in compatibility test?"

"Not predetermined," he said. "Recognised. Our finfolk scientists can confirm it through DNA once both partners consent, and there is one human lab that can now do the same, but most of us know before that. Our bodies... react. We feel it."

"React how?"

He hesitated, searching for words that wouldn't sound ridiculous. "It's a *pull*. Magnetic. A finman will always know where his mate is, without having to open his eyes. And when mates touch each other's greenskin... it's hard to describe. But it's intense. Overwhelming. If my brothers were to touch my greenskin, it feels no different from being touched elsewhere. But if a mate does it - again, I don't have words for it."

I thought of how I'd felt last night when I'd stood guard by his side. There had been this static between us, whenever I'd touched him. I'd put it down to the jellyfish reaction, but maybe... And how this morning

I'd known exactly that he was right next to me, way before I'd opened my eyes. But... No. It couldn't be.

I wasn't an alien's *mate*. I wasn't in love with him. I wasn't. Right?

I refused to examine the emotions bubbling up in me. They were caused by gratitude for him saving me from the shark. From the isolation, the drama, the injury. I felt a connection to him because we'd been isolated together on this islet. That was all. The only explanation that made sense.

"I'd like to think," I said quietly, "that you are just explaining this to teach me about your people, about the finfolk. And not because there is a bigger reason for it. But there is, isn't there?"

He smiled at me through his thick lashes. Something inside me melted. "Yes, there is. I felt it even before I first touched you. I knew it the moment I heard your voice from far away, amplified by the ocean. I've never swum so fast in my life. I had to get to you. See the person who had made me feel a connection that I had almost given up on. And then there you were, in danger, exhausted, cold, threatened by a hungry sea creature. And I knew I had to save you... but I also couldn't take you back to the island with me."

"So, this bond," I said slowly, forcing my thoughts back into order, "what does it actually do? Is it permanent? Biological imprinting or something?"

"It's permanent for us," he said. "But it needs two hearts to hold. One can sense it first; the other has to choose it. Nothing binds without consent."

"Right." I folded my arms. "Except for the part where biology is apparently making the decision for me."

"Biology doesn't decide," he said quietly. "It only tells the truth we spend our lives pretending not to feel."

"That's poetic," I muttered, "and also incredibly convenient."

His mouth twitched — almost a smile, but not quite. "You think I'd choose this?"

"Wouldn't you?"

"I've spent half my life being told I'd never have it," he said simply. "That I wasn't worthy. That my anger and pride had no place in something sacred. So yes, I would choose it — but I would never force it."

The words knocked something loose inside me. I looked away, pretending to study the horizon. The water was calm, unnervingly so. I wanted to stay calm with it, but my heart hadn't got the message.

"You're asking me to believe I'm part of some... biological recognition system," I said finally. "That out of all the people in the universe, your DNA just happens to like mine."

"It's not a coincidence," he said. "It's a connection."

I gave a short, disbelieving laugh. "Do you even hear yourself? That sounds like something off a dating app."

He shrugged, unbothered. "Maybe your people's technology is finally catching up to what ours have always known."

I wanted to argue — to call it superstition or selective memory or evolutionary nonsense — but then he looked at me, and the protest died. There was no manipulation in that gaze. Just patience, and something like awe.

"If it helps," he said softly, "you don't have to decide now. Or ever. The bond is there, yes, but it's yours to acknowledge or to walk away from. No one will take that from you."

"Including you?"

He hesitated, then nodded. "Including me."

A sigh of relief escaped me. Tension fled from my muscles, tension I hadn't even realised was there. I wasn't going to tackle the subject of do-I-want-to-be-his-girlfriend-slash-mate topic yet. There was something else simmering in my mind.

"What I don't understand," I said after a moment of silence, "is why you had to bring me here. Why isolate me? Your brothers have human mates, they could have explained the whole thing to me, told me how it was for them. This seems extreme. Possessive. Dangerous."

"I am sorry. I don't want you to think that I did this out of nefarious reasons. Let me tell you how it was for my clutch-brother, Cerban. He realised that a human female working on the island, Maelis, was his mate. He even saved her life when she got trapped in an underwater cave. And if they'd been the first finfolk-human-match to occur on the island, it would likely have all been fine. Everyone would have celebrated. But something bad had happened just a few sunpasses earlier." He took a deep breath. "I think I may have mentioned Kelon before, the male who financed our expedition to Earth? We went to the same clutch school until he was adopted by a Matriarch. He became one of the richest finmen in the city. He also became extremely self-centred and spoilt. When Elise was introduced to us by the dating agency that we'd contacted in the hope of finding eligible females, he decided to take her for himself - even though she wasn't his mate. He was greedy. Kelon kidnapped Elise and if Fionn hadn't gone after them and fought him... who knows what may have happened. Anyway, Kelon was trialled by the Intergalactic Authority and sent home to Finfolkaheem to sit out his sentence. His ship was given to Elise and luckily, the crew all decided to stay here. But ever since, the leader of the dating agency has been suspicious of us finmen. She has been insisting on following strict rules and protocols."

I held up my hand to stop his impassionate monologue.

"Wait. So you were scared of some rules? That's why you didn't bring me to the island?"

He cringed. "The rules say that humans and finmen have to stay separate until a match has been scientifically verified. It takes time for the sample to be flown to the lab, processed, analysed. If I'd taken you to the island, your injury would have been healed instantly by one of the med pods on the spaceship. You would have demanded to be taken to your ship. There would have been no reason for you to take a DNA test. You didn't know me. You'd have no reason to want to get to know me better."

He hung his head in defeat. I wanted to reach out and comfort him, but I was also angry at having the decision taken from me before I'd even known it existed.

"You still didn't tell me what happened to Cerban - was that his name?"

"Yes, Cerban. When he felt the mate bond to Maelis, he was told to stay away from her. It was awful to see him like that. A beast trapped in a cage, separated from the female he wanted to get to know. I helped them, smuggled her into his rooms while he was on house arrest. I took messages back and forth. But it was hard for both of them. She may not have felt the bond the way he did, but that didn't mean it was easy for her. It seemed to take forever until their test results finally came through, until they were finally allowed to spend time together. I hated seeing my brother in that situation. And I didn't want to be in the same situation. Not ever."

Silence followed his words. I had heard the pain, the anguish.

"I'm still not happy with your decision," I said slowly. "But I can see how what happened to your brothers affected your choices. What happens if we go to the island now? We can't stay here. Fionn said there's a storm coming."

He let out a long, deep breath. "I know. I have been ignoring the scent of the storm in the hope that it would change course. But my clutch-brother is right. We don't have a way to shelter on this islet. It is time to leave. But I will not have you swim with your injury. I will ask Fionn to get the *Tidebound* here. And then... would you like to contact your ship? The other humans? Let them know that you are alive?"

I didn't answer him right away. My mind was still stuck on the word *alive*.

A week ago, I'd have said that was obvious — of course I was alive. I had work, plans, data sets waiting for analysis, an inbox overflowing with unanswered emails. But those things belonged to another world. A smaller one. Here, stripped of everything but salt, sun, and one infuriatingly sincere alien, being alive meant something different. It meant breathing, feeling every heartbeat, acknowledging them as the small miracles they were. It meant feeling every second as it passed.

I looked at Rainse — really looked. The exhaustion on his face, the faint tension in his shoulders, the way he kept glancing at the horizon as if expecting the sea to take something else from him. He'd saved me, yes, but he'd also given me something I hadn't realised I'd lost.

Wonder.

The ocean had always been my research subject, a collection of numbers and patterns. But on this tiny island, with him, I'd remembered what had drawn me to it in the first place — the mystery, the beauty, the reminder that some things can't be measured or controlled.

I still didn't know what the bond meant for me, or what I wanted from him, exactly. I only knew that I didn't want this to end in anger. Not when there was so much more I could learn — about him, about his people, about myself.

"Yes," I said finally, meeting his eyes. "Let's contact them. The sooner we're off this island, the sooner we can figure out what comes next. And... Rainse? I will stay until we have the results of the test. I know you're worried I'll leave as soon as I'm in touch with the *Minerva*. But I promise, I won't. I'm too curious to find out if this bond is real. If it really can be scientifically explained. And I want to-" I almost didn't say it. But the words tumbled from my lips. "I want to spend more time with you."

His expression softened, relief flickering across it before he turned toward the sea.

I sat there for a moment longer, hugging my knees to my chest. The horizon had darkened, clouds gathering like a bruise over the water. Maybe a storm was coming. Or maybe it was just the world shifting again, asking me what I wanted to do with the life I'd nearly lost.

For the first time, I had an answer.

Live. Really live.

11

Rainse

The *Tidebound* descended through the clouds like a living thing. Her metal hull shimmered as the camouflage circuits disengaged, revealing curves that mimicked the shape of a breaching whale. The engines purred low and steady, stirring the sand around us into eddies. Even after all these sunpasses on Earth, watching her arrive still made my chest tighten. Spaceships were for rich people, for the elite, not for simple finmen warriors like me.

Verity stood beside me, one arm pressed against her ribs. The wind pulled at her hair, tangling it around her face, but she didn't move. She stared at the ship the way I'd once stared at the open ocean — half wonder, half disbelief.

"It looks alive," she said softly.

"She is," I murmured. "In her own way."

The *Tidebound's* underbelly opened with a hiss, lowering a landing ramp that unfurled onto the sand like a silver tongue. Water poured down its grooves, glimmering in the light. Kelon had told me once that the designers had done that on purpose — the finfolk didn't trust anything that stayed completely dry.

Verity's bare feet hesitated at the edge of the ramp. "It's... slippery."

"It adjusts," I said. "You'll be safe."

She took a tentative step forwards, then another, her balance steady despite the uneven surface. I followed a pace behind, ready to catch her if she stumbled, but she didn't. She walked straight up into the open belly of the ship, and the door sealed behind us with a soft sigh.

The temperature changed immediately. Inside, the air was cool and humid, carrying the faint scent of salt and metal polish. The floor beneath our feet curved gently, the walls smooth and rounded, lights shifting like reflected waves. Half of the corridor ahead shimmered with a thin layer of water that receded as we approached, the ship's systems recognising my dry form.

Verity's eyes were wide. "This is... incredible."

"It's home," I said quietly.

She turned toward me. "Half of it's underwater?"

"More than half," I said. "Finfolk need immersion. We don't like being away from water for too long. But some of us prefer spending some of their sunpass in air rooms, and of course some cargo would be destroyed if kept in water. A lot of the rooms inside the ship are adaptable. Wet or dry."

"Adaptable," she echoed, her gaze tracing the seams in the wall. The ship responded, dimming the lights slightly as if acknowledging her attention. She smiled faintly. "It really does feel alive."

"She likes you," I said before I could stop myself.

Verity looked at me over her shoulder, one eyebrow raised. "Ships don't like people, Rainse."

"You'd be surprised."

We reached the lift that led to the upper deck. Its door slid open with a soft ripple of sound, and I gestured for her to enter. The moment the door closed, water rose halfway up my calves while the floor beneath her stayed dry — a subtle adjustment, designed for mixed company. She watched the waterline with fascination.

"So, this is what it's like," she said quietly. "Space travel."

"Sometimes I forget that humans haven't travelled throughout the universe yet."

She laughed. "We've barely made it to our own moon. People are talking about travelling to Mars, but we don't have the technology yet to sustain human life across such distances."

"What is your ship like?" I asked.

"She's not mine. I just work on her. The *Minerva* is a research ship. A company built it and now rents it out to scientists from across the world. Lots of fancy scanners and devices, but the most used piece of technology on it is probably the coffee machine."

"You'll find better here," I said with a faint smile. "Our fabricator can make anything."

"Anything?" she asked. "Even coffee?"

"Especially coffee."

Her laughter filled the lift, bright and human. It was a sound I wanted to keep bottled somewhere safe.

The doors opened with a soft chime, revealing a wide corridor lined with doors leading to the crew quarters. The air shimmered with light from the aquaponic gardens below. Through the open archway at the far end, the medbay glowed softly, five pods arranged in a circle like sleeping pearls.

Verity hesitated again. "It's beautiful," she said. "And intimidating."

"It's both," I admitted. "Like most things worth trusting."

She looked at me then, eyes softening. "You really love it here, don't you?"

"I did," I said honestly. "Before."

"Before?"

"Before you."

The words left my mouth before I could swallow them. She froze, eyes widening, then looked away. The silence between us thickened, and I regretted the truth as soon as it was free.

"Let's get you to the medbay," I said quickly, and stepped ahead to open the door.

The medbay doors parted with a soft sigh, releasing a wave of air that smelled faintly of salt and something antiseptic yet oddly sweet. The circular room beyond gleamed under gentle light, like sunlight filtered through shallow water. Five pods curved along one side of the wall, their glass lids folded open like waiting shells.

Verity hesitated on the threshold, gaze flicking from one pod to the next. "It looks like something out of a science-fiction film."

"Science and fiction? Sounds like an oxymoron."

She laughed softly. "The science of today is tomorrow's fiction. I'm sure someone very wise and clever said that."

I stepped ahead of her. "The pod will scan you, nothing more. No pain."

"That's what every dentist says," she muttered. But she followed, cautious but curious.

The pod closest to the centre brightened as we approached, recognising her as the patient. Its inner surface shimmered, the mattress reforming into a shape that mirrored her frame. The system's voice was soft and genderless, its words translated automatically into English.

"Species: Peritan. Status: mild trauma detected. Please remove upper clothing for full analysis."

Verity blinked, colour rising in her cheeks. "It's very direct, isn't it?"

I tried not to smile. "The ship has no sense of modesty."

"Lucky ship."

She slipped off her shirt, but kept her slinky breast-harness on, and eased herself onto the mattress. The material moulded instantly around her shape, cradling her like liquid memory foam. Her hair fanned across the surface, and the soft hum of the scanners filled the air.

Lines of blue light swept across her skin, delicate as brushstrokes. The display above her pulsed gently, showing a three-dimensional outline of her body — her heart, lungs, the faint shadow where her rib had cracked.

"Fracture, minor. Surface burns, partial recovery in progress. Elevated dehydration levels. Beginning repair."

Verity tensed as a warm mist drifted over her ribs, shimmering faintly before sinking into her skin. The tension eased almost immediately, her breath deepening.

"What's it doing?" she asked.

"Sealing the break. It accelerates bone knitting and muscle regeneration," I said. "The mist carries micro-salves tailored to your chemistry."

"Feels... strange," she admitted. "Tingly. Like soda bubbles under the skin."

"That means it's working."

"Do I want to know how it knows my chemistry?"

"It sampled you the moment you walked in," I said. "This is a state of the art vessel. It's thorough."

"You don't say." Her voice was dry, but her eyes never left the display as the crack in her rib gradually faded from the hologram. The machine's hum slowed, then stopped.

"Procedure complete. Patient is stable. Recommend hydration and rest."

The lid folded open again with a soft hiss. Verity sat up carefully, running her hand down her side. "It doesn't hurt anymore."

"It won't."

"That's... incredible." She looked around, taking in the room again with new eyes. "You could heal almost anything with this."

"Almost," I said quietly. "Not everything."

Like a broken heart. Or the agony a broken bond would create.

Her gaze flicked to me, but she didn't press. She swung her legs over the side, watching the lights dim to a calmer shade of green. "How long until we reach your island?"

"We will have already landed. The *Tidebound* flies so smoothly that you don't feel landings during such a short flight."

Excitement flashed in her eyes. "That's incredible. I can't wait to meet your other brother, and of course their wives."

"Mates," I corrected gently. "Although Maelis has been talking about rings and ceremonies. I'm sure we will all learn more about human mating traditions soon."

She put her shirt back on, this time not insisting that I turn around. We both knew that I had already seen her naked, back when I'd had to take off her cold, sodden clothes. But I wouldn't mention that. I didn't want to make her uncomfortable. It had been an emergency situation. And I knew that humans were always keen to cover their bodies, not like finfolk who rarely wore more than a loincloth or wide belt around their waist.

The door slid open and Fionn poked his head inside. "Are you ready? Elise is desperate to meet you, Verity. I've called ahead to have them prepare some food for you. I don't know what you ate on that island, but I imagine it wasn't enough."

Guilt shot through me, making my stomach clench painfully. My clutch-brother was right. I hadn't looked after her properly. All she'd had to eat was fish and coconut water. I'd done a poor job caring for my mate.

"Will it be alien, I mean, finfolk food?" she asked.

"The island's chefs have started to add some of our favourite recipes to their repertoire," I said before my brother could reply. "None of those dishes will be what you'd get on Finfolkaheem, simply because we can't find the ingredients here, but some are pretty close. There is one fish species in these waters that tastes surprisingly similar to the lowoo carp back home. But if you want to try proper finfolk cuisine, I can have the fabricator prepare something for you."

"I'd like that. But not now. Now I want to see the island.

And I want to contact the *Minerva*. Let them know I'm alive and that I will be returning soon."

Fionn exchanged a stern look with me, one that meant that we'd be talking about my actions. I may be the oldest brother, but somehow, Fionn had become the one in charge.

I sighed internally and gave him an almost imperceptible nod. We'd have that discussion. But not now.

I held out an arm, smiling widely at Verity. "May I show you the island?"

She didn't hesitate as she put a hand on my arm and grinned back at me.

12

Verity

The ramp touched the sand with a soft hiss, and I stepped down into sunlight so bright it made my eyes sting. Heat rolled off the beach in shimmering waves, the air heavy with salt and the scent of wet stone. The island spread out before me like a postcard someone had left too long in the sun—edges faded, beauty a little too perfect to be real.

A line of low buildings curved along the shore, their walls pale stone and weather-softened wood, roofs thatched with palm leaves darkened by sea spray. Open verandas faced the water, framed by climbing vines and swaying ferns. Further inland, narrow paths wound through groves of coconut trees and bursts of tropical flowers, the colours almost painful after days of salt and sand.

"Welcome back to civilisation," Rainse said beside me, though there was a note in his voice that made me wonder whose civilisation he meant.

I started forward, my feet sinking into the warm sand. The air hummed with life—birds in the canopy, the distant thrum of a generator, laughter carried from somewhere near one of the smaller huts. Humans in pale uniforms moved between the huts, and tall green-skinned finfolk waded through the shallows on the far side of the bay. It was strange to see them together, sharing the same island as if it was normal to have aliens walking among humans.

"It's beautiful," I said, and meant it.

"It used to be a very rich human's island," Fionn explained from behind us. "The dating agency bought it in the hope of having a secret, secluded space to introduce matches, far away from daily life. Here, we don't have to hide. I don't know if Rainse told you, but we're working on buying another island, a bigger one, that could be a permanent home for humans and finfolk. Maybe other species as well. The Hot Tatties agency works with multiple civilisations, including Vikingar and Albyans."

That meant absolutely nothing to me. But I liked the idea of an island where aliens and humans could live together. It certainly wasn't possible in other parts of the world. As a scientist, I'd always agreed with the theory that there had to be life on other planets - the chance of Earth being the only planet where life had evolved was minuscule - but I hadn't expected that life to come and visit Earth to search for mates.

We followed a wooden walkway that curved up from the beach toward the main lodge. The boards were warm under my bare feet, smelling faintly of oil and salt. Wind chimes tinkled somewhere ahead.

A woman was waiting near the end of the path, leaning against a wooden post, sleeves rolled to her elbows. She looked instantly, unmistakably human — tanned skin, freckles across her nose, surprisingly broad shoulders. Her short hair was wind-tossed, her smile bright and genuine.

"You must be Verity," she said, pushing away from the post and offering her hand. "I'm Elise. Fionn told me he was bringing you here. Welcome to our little slice of madness."

"Thank you," I said, shaking her hand. Her grip was firm and confident. "I wasn't sure what to expect."

"Neither was I, once upon a time." Elise's grin widened as she looked at her mate. "Fionn, Rainse, Pam called, she wants you to call her back right. Cerban and Maelis are out on a dive, so you're stuck with me for the grand tour."

"I can think of worse guides," I said.

"Good answer." She gestured down the path. "Come on. You look like you could use a shower, a meal, and about twelve hours of sleep. Not necessarily in that order."

Rainse looked like he was about to say something, but then he simply nodded and followed Fionn along a path to our right.

Elise waited until they were out of earshot before whispering, "I don't know much of what's happened, Fionn only gave me a quick call to send the *Tidebound* to his location and to prepare for a new human arrival. The way Rainse looks at you, it's pretty obvious but... I mean... did he tell you? What-"

"He says I'm his mate," I blurted. I felt like laughing at how strange that sentence sounded. I still wasn't used to this talk of 'mates' rather than partners, boyfriends, husbands.

"And what do you think about that? If you don't mind me asking. You don't know me, so I won't be offended if you'd rather keep it to yourself."

"I honestly don't know. I need more time to think about it. It's been a lot, these last few days."

"I get that. And it's not like you signed up to the Hot Tatties dating agency like I did. I was prepared to find love - although I mostly did it to get away from everyday life and get a free holiday out of it. Finding Fionn was unexpected. I hadn't planned to actually fall in love." It was easy to see just how happy she was with her alien mate. I had so many questions for her - but not now. First, I wanted to see this island.

We followed the path uphill, the boards warm under my bare feet. Salt wind tugged at the hem of my loose shirt, and the rhythmic slapping of waves followed us wherever we went. The island was alive with sound — the hum of insects, the call of seabirds, the chatter of people in the distance.

Elise led with an easy confidence, clearly used to the heat. The path curved between flower beds bursting with tropical colour — scarlet hibiscus, yellow frangipani, some plant with blue trumpet-shaped blossoms that looked almost too vivid to be real. I felt like I'd been transported into a botanical garden. The air was thick with the scent of sun and greenery and distant rain.

"It's not exactly what I imagined," I admitted.

Elise laughed, the sound light and easy. "Yeah, I remember that feeling. When I came here, I thought I'd signed up for a cheeky little holiday package — cocktails, beaches, maybe a bit of romance if I was lucky. I didn't expect *space-faring mermen* and an intergalactic authority that would kidnap me to be part of an alien court case."

We followed the path as it curved inland, the trees thickening into a patch of jungle alive with sound.

Lizards darted across the boards ahead of us, their bellies flashing silver in the sun. Beyond them, a row of low stone lodges came into view — airy buildings with wide verandas and hammocks strung between the posts.

"That's the guest accommodation," Elise said. "Mostly humans, a few finfolk who like dry beds and air conditioning. The rest stay on the other side of the island near the cove — more water access, fewer rules about clothing."

I gave her a sidelong glance. "You mean they actually—"

"Oh yes," she said cheerfully. "They hate fabric. Drives the agency nuts, but you try telling a seven-foot merman he needs to wear a shirt. Not worth the argument."

I laughed, tension slipping out of me for the first time all day. "Sounds like you've adjusted."

"Took a while," she admitted. "It helps when you love one of them. And when you own the ship that got them here."

"That's yours?" I asked, glancing back toward the distant gleam of metal where the *Tidebound* rested at the end of the beach.

"Technically mine, yes." Her voice softened. "Wasn't really part of the plan, but life doesn't usually wait for plans. You'll see. Everything is different when you love an alien."

The path rose again, opening into a wide terrace lined with potted palms and driftwood benches. Beyond it, the ocean stretched endless and blue, beckoning to be explored. The whole scene shimmered with impossible calm, as if none of the chaos I'd lived through had ever happened.

"Your suite's just up there," Elise said, pointing to a bungalow shaded by bougainvillaea. "All the beach lodges are currently occupied, but this has the best view on the island, and it's close enough to the main lodge that you can grab food whenever you like. I've asked them to bring you something light — your stomach's probably still recovering."

"You've thought of everything," I said quietly.

"I've had practice," she replied. "I've been taking over more and more responsibilities here since I was kind of jobless and bored. We've had a few ladies sent here by the dating agency, with more arriving every few days. But you might be the first scientist. The others usually just wanted adventure."

"Guess I got both," I said.

She smiled and stepped aside to let me enter. The room smelled faintly of salt and lemon polish, the sheets crisp, the ceiling fan turning slow circles. For the first time in what felt like forever, I exhaled.

"Get some rest," Elise said. "There is only one more thing to discuss before I leave you in peace. Everyone on the island gets asked whether they want to do a DNA test and be added to the Hot Tatties database. Their algorithms constantly search for matches and we've had a few surprise hits recently. Cameron, one of the cooks, was matched with an Albyan two days ago and left the island yesterday to meet his match in orbit. Crazy fast."

"I suppose my encounter with an alien was even faster. He saved me from a shark attack."

Elise grinned. "I'm pretty sure the local sharks have learned by now that finmen are way stronger than them." Her smile wavered a little. "Do you want to submit a sample? Or do you want to have a think about it first?"

Part of me wanted to delay. Return to the *Minerva*, run from the situation, forget everything I had seen. But even now, I could feel that strange sensation in the centre of my chest, a gentle pull that told me exactly where on the island Rainse currently was. I was certain I could follow it and find him without getting lost. It didn't make sense. Didn't follow any scientific basis that I knew about. But as he'd said, their science was our fiction - for now. Until we developed further.

I took a deep breath. "I will take the test. But first, I have a phone call to make."

13

Rainse

F ionn's voice was calm, which was somehow worse than if he'd shouted. "You hid a human mate on an island. You didn't tell anyone."

"I didn't hide her," I said through gritted teeth. "I kept her safe."

He folded his arms. "From what? Her human colleagues and proper medical care?"

Before I could answer, the holo projector on his desk flickered, and Pam's image resolved mid-air — silver hair, immaculate suit, and the expression of a woman who'd long since stopped being impressed by excuses.

Pam's holographic image flickered in the air above Fionn's desk, crisp and businesslike — not angry, but the kind of polite that meant *someone's about to be scolded diplomatically.*

"Rainse." It was more sigh than greeting. "Why did I ever agree to working with you finmen? I've never had this kind of trouble with other aliens. True, the Vikingar have no table manners and the Albyans have no sense of personal space, but you boys... Do you think I have nothing better to do than deal with yet another rule breaker?"

I tried to look guilty and demure. I wasn't sure I succeeded. I could feel my mate moving further away from me, and it took all my navy-trained self-discipline not to run out of the room and find her. Tell her just what I felt for her. That it wasn't just the bond that brought us together. That it was so much more. I would want her to be mine even without the bond. I had never been more certain about anything. I loved the way she looked at the world, with the mind of a scientist. I loved her laugh, that little giggle sound when she smiled. I loved her resilience, her strength. I loved her bravery, how she hadn't hesitated diving into a crowd of stinging creatures that had disabled me. I loved...her.

"Are you listening to me?" Pam asked sternly.

"Yes. No. Pam, I'm sorry, but there is nothing much to say. She is my mate. I know she is. She feels it as well. And once she's done a DNA test and has been added to your database, the whole world will know it. Why do we have to wait? Why do you have to separate us when it is obvious that we are meant to be together?"

Fionn put a calming hand on my shoulder. "Rainse..."

"Who said anything about separating you?" Pam asked, one immaculately shaped eyebrow pulled up.

"I assumed... Cerban..."

"We have learned much from how we handled Cerban and Maelis. Hot Tatties is a dating agency, not the police. Yes, we work with the permission of the Intergalactic Authority, but as long as we keep them informed and don't allow random aliens to join the database, we pretty much have free rein on how we operate. Keeping Cerban and Maelis separate was... not the best decision. I see that now, with hindsight. But back then, it was done in order to protect Maelis and other women. Now that we have realised that Kelon was an isolated case, that the majority of finmen are honourable, kind males who would never think to hurt a female, we can change our policies somewhat."

"So you'll let us be together? Now?"

I couldn't believe what I was hearing. After they'd forced my brother and his mate to stay apart for many sunpasses, they were offering me the opposite? It didn't make sense. Not that I was about to complain.

"It is the woman's decision. If - what is her name?"

"Verity," I said quickly.

"If Verity explicitly says that this is her choice, that she was not coerced or forced in any way, then we can house the two of you in the same building. Maybe not the same room quite yet, however. Baby steps. And if she wants to submit a sample, I'll fast-track it through the lab. Trust me, I'm as curious as you are to find out if you accidentally found your mate. I mean, what are the chances? It is fascinating. Almost makes you believe in fate..."

As soon as the call ended, I was out of the room, leaving Fionn to deal with the practicalities. I had to see her. Fionn shouted after me, but I ignored him.

The moment I stepped outside, the bond flared — clear, strong, alive. She was close. Not afraid, not angry. Just restless. Like the ocean before a change in tide.

I followed the pull through the palm-lined paths, past the soft hum of the resort. The air was heavy with heat and the scent of salt and sweet alien flowers, the kind of afternoon that promised rain but hadn't decided when.

And then I saw her.

Verity stood at the water's edge, the sunlight catching her hair, turning it to copper fire. She turned before I spoke, as though she'd felt me coming — maybe she had. I hoped so. It meant she felt the bond the same way I did.

"I thought you'd be in trouble," she said, shading her

eyes against the glare. "I expected someone to come and tell me that I couldn't see you for a while."

"I was suitably admonished," I admitted. "Pam said I'm officially on her list."

"That doesn't sound good."

"She has many lists." I smiled. "I think this one's called 'Finmen Who Give Me Grey Hairs.'"

That made her laugh — soft, real, the kind of sound I'd been chasing since I first pulled her from the sea.

I stopped a few paces away. "She said something else, though. Something I didn't expect."

"Oh?"

"She's willing to let us stay near each other. As long as you agree to it. Your choice."

Verity blinked, clearly taken aback. "She... actually said that?"

"She did."

Her gaze flicked over my face, as if looking for the trick. Finding none, her shoulders eased. "That's... surprisingly reasonable."

I took a step closer, careful not to crowd her. The sun was warm on our skin, the sea whispering against the sand. "I told her what I know. That you're my mate."

Her lips parted slightly. "You're very sure of that."

"I've never been more sure of anything."

A pause — long enough for a gull to cry overhead, long enough for the air between us to shift.

"When I'm near you," she said quietly, "everything feels... quieter. Easier."

"That's what the bond does," I said. "But it's also what *you* do."

Her laugh came out breathless. "That's either the most romantic or most confusing thing anyone's ever said to me."

"Then let me try something simpler."

I reached out, brushed my fingers along her cheek. Her skin was warm, her breath catching just once — and the bond surged, bright and electric, as if the sea itself was holding its breath.

"Do you feel it?" I whispered.

"Yes," she breathed. "I don't understand it, but yes."

"Then stop trying to understand."

The pull between us snapped taut, invisible but unbreakable, humming with the same low power that lives in the sea before a storm. She shivered, though the sun was still warm, her lips parting on a breath that trembled somewhere between disbelief and invitation.

I cupped her face, my thumb tracing the line of her jaw. Her pulse beat fast against my palm — quick, human, alive. When our eyes met, I saw the question there, the choice. She didn't move away.

So I closed the distance.

The first touch was light, a test. A whisper of contact that sent electricity racing through me. Her breath hitched. Mine stopped altogether. For a heartbeat, it was just that — shared air, shared silence. Then she made a sound, small and uncertain, and tilted her head the slightest fraction closer.

That was all it took.

I deepened the kiss, letting instinct guide me. She tasted of salt and sun, of the ocean that had given her to me. The world tilted — the sand beneath us, the endless horizon, the rush of waves that rose and fell in time with the pounding of our hearts. She gripped my shoulders, pulling me down to her level, and I went willingly.

The bond roared to life. Not the faint hum I'd felt before, but a surge — light and heat flooding through every part of me. It was too much and not enough, both wild and inevitable, the ocean itself surging through our veins. She gasped against my mouth, but she didn't pull away. Her fingers slid up my neck, tangling in my hair, holding me there as though afraid I'd vanish if she let go.

I kissed her again, slower this time, savouring the way she sighed into it, the way her lips softened against mine. Every sound — the seabirds, the waves, the whisper of palms — faded into nothing. There was only her. The taste of her, the rhythm of her breath, the heat that bloomed between us like sunlight through water.

When I finally drew back, the world was shimmering. Her eyes were still closed, her lips still parted. She looked dazed — no, *alive*.

"That was..." she began, voice catching.

I brushed my thumb over her lower lip, barely breathing. "Yes," I said quietly. "It was."

Her eyes opened, and what I saw there stole whatever composure I'd managed to hold on to. Wonder. Fear. Want.

"Pam's going to hate this," she whispered, and that tiny, breathless laugh of hers broke the spell just enough for me to smile.

"She'll live."

And then I kissed her again — because stopping felt impossible, and because for the first time since I'd left Finfolkaheem, I knew exactly where I belonged.

14

I couldn't believe I'd kissed him. I couldn't believe how good it had felt. And how much I wanted to do it again, and again, until my lips were swollen and I couldn't remember my own name.

It wasn't supposed to happen like that. Nothing about this was supposed to happen like that. One minute, I'd been trying to reason with myself, listing every sensible reason not to want him — alien, abductor, wrong species, wrong situation — and the next, his mouth was on mine, and my body had voted for complete mutiny.

I pressed my fingers to my lips. They still tingled. My pulse hadn't slowed; it was thudding hard enough that I could feel it everywhere — in my ribs, my throat, the tips of my fingers. The sea breeze cooled my skin but couldn't calm the heat that had taken root beneath it.

I'd kissed men before.

But never like that.

There'd been no hesitation, no polite test of compatibility, no trying to make it *work*. It had just... worked. Instantly. Like my body already knew the rhythm of his, like some deep, ancient part of me had been waiting for that precise moment to exist.

I wanted to blame it on the bond — that strange biological phenomenon he'd described, part chemistry, part instinct. Maybe it explained the attraction, the dizzying pull between us. Maybe it was his scent, or pheromones, or whatever mysterious evolutionary quirk made our DNA spark like flint.

But science didn't explain the way his touch had made me *feel*.

I'd spent years studying patterns — migration routes, sonar communication, the subtle logic behind animal behaviour. None of it had prepared me for this. For him.

I turned toward the sea. The waves were calm again, stretching out in endless shades of silver-blue. He was somewhere behind me, probably just as dazed as I was. Maybe not — Finfolk were used to the idea of "fated mates." Maybe this was ordinary for him. Another biological inevitability.

But for me? It felt anything but ordinary.

I closed my eyes and tried to breathe, to analyse, to think. The scientist in me demanded structure — cause, effect, explanation. The woman in me only wanted to feel the next kiss.

Maybe both were right.

"You're thinking very loudly," he said.

I smiled without opening my eyes. "Occupational hazard. Scientists overanalyse everything."

He came to stand beside me, close but not touching. The restraint in that was almost unbearable. "Do you regret it?"

I turned to face him. The sunlight caught the faint shimmer of his greenskin, the subtle movement of it in the wind, like kelp swaying under a current. He looked impossibly beautiful — familiar and strange all at once.

"No," I said honestly. "That's the problem."

Something flickered across his expression — relief, maybe, or hunger. "Good."

I shook my head, half laughing, half on the edge of another disaster. "You can't just— you can't kiss me like that and expect me to think straight."

"I wasn't expecting you to think at all," he said softly.

And there it was again — that quiet confidence, the heat beneath the calm. I wanted to be angry at him for it, but I couldn't. He wasn't playing a game. He was just being *honest*.

The bond pulsed between us, low and steady. I wondered if he felt it the same way I did — like standing on the edge of a cliff, knowing that jumping would feel like flying, even if you might drown after.

"I need time," I said finally. "To understand what this is."

He nodded once, solemn. "You'll have it. I'll wait as long as it takes."

I believed him. That was the terrifying part.

When he turned back toward the resort, the sunlight caught him again — scales glinting, shoulders broad, strength and softness in equal measure. I watched him go, my heart a chaotic mess of logic and longing.

I had every reason to walk away.

And not a single desire to do it.

I somehow made it back to my bungalow before the emotions caught up with me.

Inside, I closed the door and leaned against it, pressing my fingers to my lips. They still tingled from his kiss.

What was I doing?

I walked to the window and stared out at the ocean.

Somewhere out there was the *Minerva*. My colleagues. My research. The life I'd spent years building.

And I was ready to throw it away for an alien I'd known for less than a week.

Was I insane?

I pulled out the tablet I'd been given and scrolled through my emails. Dozens of messages. Questions about data. A reminder about the conference paper I was supposed to submit next month. An email from my university supervisor asking how the expedition was going.

My life. My real life.

I sat on the edge of the bed and made myself think it through.

The facts: I'd nearly died. Been rescued by an alien. Been kept on an island against my will—no, that wasn't fair. He'd protected me when I was injured. There was a difference.

But was there?

He'd made choices for me. Decided I couldn't handle the swim. Decided I needed to be kept separate from everyone else until... what? Until I fell for him?

And I had. That was the terrifying part.

One kiss and I was ready to upend my entire existence.

The bond hummed in my chest, a gentle pull telling me exactly where he was on the island. Two buildings away. Probably worrying about me. Probably waiting.

Was this love? Or just very sophisticated biochemistry?

I thought about my mother, who'd always said she knew my father was the one the moment she met him. "Just knew," she'd said, as if that explained everything.

I'd never believed in that. Love at first sight. Instant connections. Soulmates.

But I'd never met an alien before who talked about bonds and fated mates.

I looked at my reflection in the mirror. Same face. Same eyes. But something had changed. I looked... alive. More alive than I'd felt in years.

Was that the bond? Or was it him?

Did it matter?

The scientist in me screamed yes. Understanding the mechanism mattered. Knowing whether I was being influenced mattered. Having control over my own choices mattered.

But the woman who'd kissed him, who'd felt that surge of rightness, who right now wanted nothing more than to do it again... she didn't care about mechanisms.

She just wanted him.

I pressed my hand to my chest, feeling my own heartbeat. Steady. Sure.

I could leave. Contact the *Minerva*. Say this was all too much, too fast, too alien. Go back to my research and my papers and my carefully planned career.

Or I could stay. Take the DNA test. See if the bond was real. Give this—give him—a chance.

The pull in my chest strengthened, as if the bond itself was voting.

But that wasn't fair. The bond didn't get to decide. I did.

So what did I want?

I closed my eyes and let myself really feel it. Not the bond. Not the biology. Just... what my heart wanted when I stripped away all the fear and logic and doubt.

I wanted to learn his language. Hear him sing the currents. Wake up to greenskin wrapped around me like a living blanket. Argue with him about scientific method. Kiss him until we both forgot our own names.

I wanted him.

Not because of the bond. Because of who he was. Who we could be together.

The realization settled over me like calm water.

I opened my eyes and looked at my phone one more time. The *Minerva* could wait. The conference could wait. Everything could wait.

This—him—couldn't.

I stood up, smoothed down my borrowed clothes, and headed for the door.

Time to stop running from what I wanted.

I found him walking along the beach, guided to him by the bond.

"Wait!"

He stopped immediately, turning to me, the sunlight catching the fine sheen of water still clinging to his greenskin. His eyes met mine, unreadable but patient, as if he'd been waiting for me to come running back all along.

I swallowed hard. "Have you eaten yet?"

His head tilted slightly. "No. I can't even remember when I last had some food. Why?"

"Because I haven't either," I said, surprised by how steady my voice sounded. "Well, nothing but a banana from the fruit basket in my room. And I thought... maybe we could fix that. Together."

For a heartbeat, he just looked at me — silent, assessing, as though trying to decide if this was real. Then the corners of his mouth curved, and his entire face lit up. "You're asking me to dinner."

"Yes." I folded my arms, mostly because I didn't know what to do with my hands. "It's called a date. Humans do that sometimes when they're trying to make sense of whatever this is. When they want to get to know each other further, on neutral ground, in a nice place."

"I know what a date is," he said, and there was a faint glimmer of amusement in his eyes. "I just didn't think you'd want one with me."

"I didn't either," I admitted. "And yet, here we are."

That made him smile, and it was devastating. The kind of smile that felt like sunlight breaking through water.

"Then it would be my honour," he said simply.

The ridiculous formality of it made me laugh — a small, unsteady sound that somehow grounded me. "Good. I saw a dining area near the main lodge when Elise showed me around. I'm guessing they serve more than fish?"

"They will make you whatever you want. By now the entire island will know that you almost drowned and then almost became shark food. You'll be the local celebrity and favourite source of gossip for a few sunpasses, before they move on to a new target. I recommend you milk it while you can."

I laughed. "I guess there's a lot of gossip on an island like this."

"You have no idea."

We fell into step together as we made our way up the beach, the silence between us comfortable this time. I was aware of him in that hyper-focused way that made everything else blur — his scent, the quiet rhythm of his breathing, the faint rustle of his greenskin as he moved.

When we reached the boardwalk, the air shifted again — cooler, carrying the faint aromas of spice and citrus from the kitchen. A handful of human and finfolk couples were scattered at the tables under wide canopies, the atmosphere relaxed, private. We gained a few curious glances, but they tried to pretend not to notice us.

A hostess — human, with a wide smile and beautifully braided black hair — greeted us with the polite warmth of someone trained to ignore the extraordinary. "Table for two?"

"Yes," I said before Rainse could. "Somewhere quiet, if possible."

She led us to a table near the edge of the terrace, overlooking the lagoon. The light was golden, the sky stretching wide and endless above the sea. I sat down, half afraid the spell would break once we were seated like normal people doing normal things. But it didn't.

Rainse watched me across the table, his expression soft but intent. "This is your idea of an experiment, isn't it?"

"Maybe." I picked up the menu, mostly to have something to hold. "Observation through participation."

"Then I'm honoured to be your subject," he said.

"Don't get ahead of yourself," I replied dryly, but I couldn't quite hide my smile.

The waitress appeared with two glasses of cold water, and I took a sip before glancing back at him. "I don't know how this ends, Rainse. I don't even know what happens next."

He reached across the table, not touching me, just close enough for his fingers to rest on the wood between us. "Then let's just start with dinner."

"I can do that. When you eat here, do you usually choose human or finfolk food?"

"I like to mix it up. To be fair, most of the finfolk options have been humanised because of lack of ingredients. But if you're looking for a recommendation, the Tw'li fish soup is quite authentic."

"I think I've had enough fish for a while, but thank you. I feel like carbs. Lots of carbs."

He laughed softly, then his expression suddenly soured. "I'm sorry I didn't look after you properly while you were on the little island. I should have known that just fish and coconuts wasn't good enough. I should have-"

I put a finger to my lips. "What's done is done. Let's focus on the present rather than the past. As long as that in future, you only whisk me away to tropical islands if I explicitly ask for it."

"I promise," he said solemnly.

The waitress arrived to take our orders. Overwhelmed with the amount of options on the menu, I made it easy for myself and went with the chef's special vegetarian menu - mostly to avoid fish. To my surprise, Rainse only chose human dishes. Curious. Maybe he was trying to impress me.

We chatted while we waited for our starter. Inconsequential topics, yet it felt natural and cosy. As if we'd done this many times before. I liked being in his company. I was almost annoyed when our starters arrived, even though my stomach was clenching with hunger.

He didn't touch his food at first. He just watched me, a little too intently, as if trying to memorise my features. When I caught him, he looked faintly guilty and reached for his own plate.

"I contacted the *Minerva* earlier," I said after enjoying a few spoonfuls of soup. "It was really good to speak to my team."

His gaze sharpened. "They know you're safe?"

"Yes. And they found Hugo and Jammie." Relief softened my voice; I hadn't realised how much weight I'd been carrying until it eased. "Hugo was picked up by a trawler not far from where we went down. He's bruised, dehydrated, but alive. Jammie was hypothermic and delirious, but recovered quickly. The *Minerva* is currently docked so they could get hospital treatment. They asked whether I'd want them to arrange transport back to the ship for me. I didn't know what to say. I had to pretend that I couldn't quite remember how I'd got to this island. They wouldn't have believed the truth. I didn't like lying to them, but it was the only way."

He opened his mouth as if to say something, but stayed quiet, waiting for me to talk through the situation.

"I miss them. I miss my research. But at the same time... I don't want this adventure to end quite yet. I don't want to return to the *Minerva* and continue as if nothing happened, as if we..."

"As if we didn't happen," he whispered.

"Exactly. I wish you could come on board with me, but I know that's impossible. You'd become the topic of research, not the cetaceans. They said they'd be docked for another two days or so, to make sure Hugo and Jammie are fully recovered. Then they need a response."

"I would love to see you do your science. But I agree, I have to stay on this island. We are not allowed to reveal our existence to other humans."

"My research feels small now," I admitted quietly. "Hours and hours of data about whales, tracking patterns, behavioural analysis... It all seemed so important. But after nearly drowning, I can't stop thinking about how much I don't know. About how much there is down there we've never even touched."

"Your kind looks at the sea and sees mystery," he said. "Mine looks and sees home. But maybe they are the same thing."

I smiled at that. "Spoken like a poet."

He tilted his head. "We call them song-scholars. On Finfolkaheem, every scientist learns to sing the currents before they study them. You can't measure the ocean unless you've listened to it first."

"That's beautiful," I said softly.

"It's practical," he said with a half-smile. "But I like that you think otherwise."

For a while, we ate in comfortable silence, the soft murmur of other diners fading beneath the sound of the tide. I couldn't remember the last time a conversation had felt so easy, so natural.

When I glanced at him again, he was already looking at me — not staring, not intense, just *looking*.

"I'm glad you got to speak to your people," he said. "Even if it means you might leave."

"I haven't decided anything yet," I said truthfully.

"Then I'll hope."

"You seem to do a lot of that," I teased gently.

He smiled — the kind that started in his eyes. "Only since you arrived."

15

Rainse

The world was quieting in preparation for the oncoming storm by the time we left the restaurant. The last light of the sun painted everything gold — the sand, the palms, her skin. A warm breeze lifted the edge of her hair, and I had to curl my fingers into fists to stop myself from brushing it back.

"Too full?" I asked as we followed the boardwalk toward the beach.

She gave me a lazy smile. "You're the one who convinced me to try seaweed pudding."

"It's a delicacy," I said.

"It's green jelly with ideas above its station," she replied.

I laughed, the sound startlingly easy. "Then perhaps I owe you something better to end the night."

"Oh? And what do Finfolk consider better?"

"At home, we'd swim. But with you, I propose a walk," I said. "No pudding. No talking if you don't want to."

Her smile softened. "Walking sounds good."

We slipped off the boardwalk and onto the cool sand. The sea was starting to get rougher, the sky turning that impossible shade between blue and silver that happens just before the stars appear. I listened to the rhythm of her breathing beside me, the quiet crunch of our steps.

For the first time in mooncrossings, I wasn't thinking about rules or reputation or suppressed needs. Just her.

"You're quiet," she said after a while.

"Thinking."

"About?"

"You," I admitted. "And how easily you fit here. How easily you fit anywhere."

She looked at me out of the corner of her eye. "That's funny. I've never felt like I fit anywhere."

"You do now."

The wind lifted between us, warm and scented with salt and oncoming rain. She stopped walking, turning to face the sea, and I stopped too.

"Do you ever miss your world?" she asked.

"Every day," I said honestly. "But I think what I really miss is the way I *used* to belong there. My life with my clutch-brothers, innocent and full of joy. Before the Matriarchs decided who was worthy of love and who wasn't."

Her voice softened. "You mean before they told you that you couldn't have a mate."

I nodded. "It's strange. I used to think it was punishment. Now I think it was preparation."

"For me?" she teased gently.

"For this," I said. "For meeting someone who wouldn't believe in fate, but would still choose me."

Something flickered across her face — surprise, emotion, maybe both. She didn't speak. Instead, she reached out and took my hand. The gesture was simple, but it felt important.

We walked like that until the first stars appeared. The bond pulsed quietly between us, steady as a heartbeat.

When the air shifted, I noticed it first — the faint crackle that always came before a storm. Clouds were gathering over the horizon, the kind that moved quickly in these latitudes.

"We should head back," I said, but she didn't move.

"I like it," she said softly. "The air feels alive."

"So do you," I murmured.

Her gaze lifted to mine, and the look there undid me. All the restraint, the waiting, the careful distance — gone.

I stepped closer, close enough to feel her breath against my throat. She didn't step back. Her fingers slid down my arm, finding the faint texture of my greenskin where it curled around my wrist. The touch sent heat rippling through me.

"Rainse..."

"Tell me to stop," I said, my voice rougher than I intended.

She didn't. Instead, she rose onto her toes and kissed me.

It wasn't the desperate rush of before — this one burned slower, deeper. The taste of her filled me, warm and salt-sweet. I kissed her back with all the patience I'd been forcing into words these last few days, and all the want I couldn't hide anymore.

The first rumble of thunder rolled across the sea.

She broke the kiss long enough to whisper, "We should probably find shelter."

"There's an abandoned hut past the grove," I said, already taking her hand. "Come."

She didn't argue.

We ran, laughing when the first heavy drops of rain hit the sand, our fingers locked tight. By the time we reached the small wooden building at the edge of the beach, the storm had arrived in full — warm rain drumming on the roof, wind tearing through the palms outside.

Inside, the air was dim, smelling faintly of salt and wood polish. She stood in the doorway, rainwater glistening on her skin, hair plastered to her cheeks.

She looked like the sea come to life.

And I couldn't look away. She was everything I'd ever dreamed of. And yet, if I wasn't careful, I may lose the most precious person I had ever met. I couldn't pressure her. Had to take it slow. Had to let her make the decisions.

I forced myself to look around the small hut. It was mostly empty, except for a stack of towels near the door, a heap of seat cushions and a random assortment of bottles.

Rain drummed against the roof, steady and hypnotic. The single light in the hut flickered, throwing soft shadows across the walls. Verity wrung the water from her hair and laughed quietly, breathless from the run.

"You weren't kidding about the storm," she said.

"It came faster than I expected." I reached for a towel and offered it to her.

She took it, smiling. "How very convenient. I wonder if any of these bottles are still full. The wine at dinner was nice, but I wouldn't say no to a nice gin."

"I don't believe I know what gin is."

"I will make sure to introduce you. If there's none in here, we'll get some at the bar. Once the storm has calmed down. I don't want to get wet again. Do you like storms?" She rubbed the towel through her hair and I stood there, mesmerised.

"I respect them. They remind you how small you are."

She hummed, a thoughtful sound. "I used to love them. When I was little, we'd go on holiday to the south of France. Lots of thunderstorms there in the summer. I'd sit by the window and count the seconds between lightning and thunder. But now, after the whale incident... they just make me think of waves."

I wanted to reach for her but didn't. Not yet. "You were brave, Verity. You didn't just survive — you fought the sea and won."

She glanced up, eyes catching the dim light. "You make it sound heroic. I think I was just lucky. And you did most of the heavy lifting."

"Luck doesn't swim toward danger to save someone

else," I said softly. "I may have saved you at first, but it was you who saved my life in return."

Her lips parted slightly, but she didn't answer.

Thunder cracked overhead, shaking the wooden beams. She jumped, and I stepped closer on instinct. "Easy," I murmured.

"I'm fine," she said, though her voice was tight.

"You don't have to be. I get jumpy sometimes, too."

For a long moment, neither of us moved. The storm howled outside, all noise and fury, but in here everything felt suspended — as if the world was holding its breath.

She exhaled first. "This place smells like varnish."

"Better than fish."

That earned a laugh. "You know, you're not what I expected."

"What did you expect?"

She tilted her head, studying me. "Honestly? Something with tentacles. Or more eyes. I never imagined aliens would look so... human. Or so..."

"So what?" I asked, stepping a little closer.

Her lips curved. "Attractive."

I raised an eyebrow. "Attractive," I repeated slowly. "That's a compliment, yes?"

"Don't let it go to your head," she said, though the corners of her mouth betrayed her.

Her fingers lingered against the edge of my greenskin, tracing the delicate fronds where they fanned out from my ribs. The contact was feather-light, curious — but my body reacted as if she'd set fire to it. Had I warned her what touching my greenskin would do to me? I couldn't remember.

The greenskin flared in response, its surface shifting, alive beneath her touch. I drew in a sharp breath. My mind was empty. All blood suddenly seemed to rush to my cock.

She froze. "Did I hurt you?"

"No," I managed, voice low and rough. "Just... surprised me."

"It moved," she whispered, watching it shimmer faintly in the dim light.

"It reacts to touch," I said carefully. "Usually water currents, temperature shifts... or—" I swallowed, struggling for words that didn't sound like begging, "— mates."

Her eyes met mine. There was understanding there now, and something else — interest.

"Oh," she said softly. "So it's... sensitive."

I groaned. "That's one way to put it."

I could feel the bond pulsing through me, stronger with every breath, calling to her, to this connection. Every instinct I had screamed to close the distance between us, to let her explore, to let this become what it was always meant to be.

But I forced myself to stay still. "Verity," I said quietly. "You should stop."

She didn't.

Her touch grew surer, fingertips trailing slowly along the edge of my greenskin where it curved over my shoulder. The reaction was immediate — a rush of heat, every nerve alive, every thought wiped clean except her.

"You really want me to stop?" she asked, her voice barely above the sound of the rain.

I met her gaze, breathing unsteady. "No."

That single word hung between us, heavy and certain.

Her hand slipped lower, resting against my chest where the green met blue. The bond surged, raw and undeniable, and whatever restraint I'd been clinging to shattered.

I caught her wrist gently, not to stop her, but to ground myself. "You have no idea what you're doing to me."

Her lips curved, a small, knowing smile. "I think I'm starting to."

Thunder rolled outside, distant but echoing through the walls. The storm was right above us, but our own storm was only just beginning.

16

Verity

The rain hammered against the roof like a thousand impatient fingers. Inside the hut, the air had thickened with heat and something else—something that made every breath feel significant.

My hand was still resting against Rainse's chest, fingertips tracing the edge of his greenskin. The texture was unlike anything I'd ever touched—smooth as kelp but alive, responding to me with tiny shivers and pulses. Each time I moved my fingers, his breathing hitched.

"You're staring," I whispered.

"You're touching me."

"Should I stop?"

"If you do, I might actually die." His voice came out rough, almost desperate. "And after surviving jellyfish, that would be embarrassing."

I couldn't help but laugh. "Can't have that."

I stepped closer, eliminating what little space remained between us. My other hand came up to rest against his shoulder, fingers sliding along the greenskin there. The fronds responded immediately, unfurling toward my touch like flowers seeking sunlight. Fascinating. Beautiful. Impossibly intimate.

He groaned, a sound that did things to my insides I wasn't prepared for. "Verity—"

"I know what I'm doing," I said softly, though that was only partially true. "Or at least, I'm choosing to do it. Isn't that what matters?"

"Yes." He caught my face between his hands, thumbs brushing my cheekbones with a gentleness that made my throat tight. "But I need you to be sure. Once we—if we—the bond will—"

"Will what?" I searched his eyes, seeing want and worry in equal measure. "Lock in? Become permanent? Make me crave seaweed pudding?"

Despite everything, he laughed. "The last one is irreversible, I'm afraid."

"I'll risk it."

Then I kissed him, and thinking became impossible.

This kiss was different from the ones before. Those had been tentative, exploratory—two people testing the waters. This was a dive into the deep. His mouth opened against mine, and I tasted salt and something faintly sweet, like ocean spray mixed with honey. His hands slid into my damp hair, angling my head so he could kiss me deeper, harder, until we were both breathing in gasps.

The greenskin beneath my palms started to glow faintly—a soft bioluminescence that pulsed in rhythm with his heartbeat. Or maybe mine. I couldn't tell anymore where I ended and he began.

"That's new," I managed between kisses.

"That's you," he murmured against my mouth. "It only does that for—"

"Mates," I finished. "I assumed."

"And you're okay with that?"

I pulled back just enough to meet his eyes. They were dark and endless like the bottom of the sea. "I spent my whole life studying the ocean," I said. "Trying to understand it, measure it, explain it. But some things aren't meant to be understood. They're meant to be felt."

His expression softened into something that looked like

wonder. "That's the least scientific thing I've ever heard you say."

"Don't get used to it." I tugged him back down. "I'm sure I'll have regrets in the morning. Probably involving spreadsheets."

"I'll risk it," he said, echoing my words, and kissed me again.

"Rainse," I said, the practical part of my brain fighting through the haze of desire. "I need to know—protection. I'm not on birth control anymore."

He went still. "Finfolk males are made sterile at puberty. A reversible treatment, but it requires specific intervention to undo. I can't get you pregnant. Not without hormone therapy I haven't received."

"The Matriarchs' doing?"

"Yes. Control over reproduction." His jaw tightened. "But in this case, it means you're safe."

"Okay." I exhaled. "Okay, good."

His hands moved to my waist, fingers splaying wide against my wet shirt. Even through the fabric, his touch burned. I made a frustrated sound and pulled back just long enough to yank the shirt over my head. It hit the floor with a wet slap.

Rainse went very still, his gaze tracking over my

exposed skin with an intensity that made heat pool low in my belly.

"You're staring again," I said, though my voice came out shakier than intended.

"You're perfect."

"I'm soaking wet and covered in goosebumps."

"Yes," he agreed, voice dropping an octave. "Perfect."

Before I could respond, he closed the distance between us, his mouth finding mine with a hunger that stole my breath. His hands slid up my ribs, thumbs brushing the underside of my breasts through the thin fabric of my bra, and I arched into the touch with a gasp.

"This," he murmured against my lips, fingers finding the clasp. "Off. Now."

"Impatient?"

"Desperate." His voice was rough, almost broken. "I've been imagining this since I first pulled you from the water."

The confession sent a spike of heat through me. "That's very inappropriate timing."

"I'm aware." The clasp gave way and he pulled the bra free, tossing it aside without looking. His gaze dropped, and the sound he made was purely animal. "Verity..."

Then his mouth was on my breast, hot and demanding, and I stopped thinking entirely. His tongue circled my nipple before he sucked hard enough to make my knees buckle. Only his arm around my waist kept me upright.

"Rainse—" His name came out as a moan.

"Tell me what you want," he said against my skin, his free hand sliding down to work at my trousers.

"You. I want you."

"Be more specific." His fingers found the button, popped it open. "I want to hear you say it."

My brain struggled to form words while his hand slipped inside my trousers, fingers teasing along the edge of my underwear. "I want... God, I want you inside me."

"Better." The trousers hit the floor, followed immediately by my underwear, and suddenly I was completely bare while he was still half-dressed. The inequality should have bothered me, but the way he looked at me—like I was something precious and profane all at once—made me feel powerful instead of vulnerable.

He dropped to his knees in front of me.

"What are you—oh—"

His mouth found the inside of my thigh, kissing and biting a path upward. The greenskin along his shoulders brushed against my legs, and the sensation was unlike anything I'd ever felt—electric and alive, reading every shiver and gasp.

"I've wanted to taste you," he said, breath hot against my skin, "since you first touched my greenskin. Do you know what that did to me? How badly I wanted to—"

His tongue found me, and the rest of his words dissolved into action.

I grabbed his shoulders for balance, fingers digging into the greenskin there. It pulsed beneath my palms in rhythm with what his mouth was doing, as if it was responding to my pleasure. The dual sensation—his tongue circling my clit, the greenskin vibrating against my hands—was almost too much.

"Oh God—Rainse—"

He hummed against me, the vibration sending sparks up my spine, and added his fingers. One, then two, curling inside me with devastating precision. The greenskin along his arms extended, tendrils wrapping gently around my thighs, holding me open for him.

"That's—that's not fair—" I gasped.

He pulled back just long enough to say, "Fair?" His fingers continued their movement, finding a spot inside me that made my vision blur. "I'm not trying to be fair. I'm trying to make you come so hard you forget your own name."

Then his mouth returned to my clit, sucking hard while his fingers moved faster, and the greenskin pulsed and the whole world narrowed to the coil of pleasure tightening in my core until—

I shattered, crying out his name, my legs shaking so badly he had to catch me. He gentled me through it, his movements slowing, tongue soft and soothing until I could breathe again.

"Okay?" he asked, pressing a kiss to my hip.

"I—" My voice didn't work properly. "That was—you can't just—"

"Use your words, scientist."

I grabbed his hair and pulled him up to kiss him, tasting myself on his tongue. "Bed. Cushions. Whatever. Now."

He smiled against my mouth. "Demanding."

"You started it."

In one fluid movement, he lifted me—easily, as if I weighed nothing—and I wrapped my legs around his waist on instinct. The cushions were suddenly beneath my back, soft and ridiculous, and he was above me, still wearing that damned belt.

"Off," I demanded, tugging at it. "This needs to be off."

"Allow me." He reached down and released the clasp himself. The belt fell away, and—

"Oh," I said stupidly.

His cock was magnificent and utterly alien. The base was a rich kelp green that deepened gradually toward the head—an oceanic blue that glistened like wet stone. But it was the movement that made my breath catch. Thick ridges pulsed just beneath the surface, moving in a wave-like rhythm even though he wasn't touching it.

"It's..." I couldn't find words.

"Different," he finished, a hint of uncertainty in his voice.

"Beautiful," I corrected, reaching out tentatively. "Can I?"

He nodded, jaw tight.

When my fingers wrapped around him, the skin rippled beneath my touch—the ridges moving up and down like waves on a beach. The sensation was hypnotic, alive. Below, I could see the smooth, tight skin of his scrotum, and I counted—

"Three?" I asked, surprised into scientific observation even now.

"Is that a problem?" His voice was strained.

"No, it's—" I stroked him experimentally, watching the ridges pulse faster. "Fascinating. Do you control this? The movement?"

"A little." His hips jerked into my hand. "But once I'm inside you, I'll lose all control. The ridges will move on their own, responding to—oh fuck—"

I'd squeezed gently, thumb brushing over the blue head. "Responding to what?"

"To your pleasure." He caught my wrist, stopping me. "Verity, if you keep doing that, this will end embarrassingly fast."

"Will you fit?" The question came out more uncertain than I intended.

His expression softened. "We're compatible. The bond wouldn't exist otherwise. And the greenskin will help. Trust me?"

I guided him to my entrance, lifting my hips in invitation. "Show me."

He pushed inside in one slow, devastating thrust.

The stretch was intense—almost too much—but the greenskin was already responding, secreting something slick and warm that eased the way. And those ridges—God, those ridges. They moved inside me, pulsing against my inner walls in that same wave-like rhythm, hitting spots I didn't know existed.

"Oh fuck," I gasped. "That's—you're—"

"Good?" he gritted out, barely holding still.

"Move. Please move. I need—"

He withdrew slowly, and the ridges dragged against me, creating friction that made my toes curl. Then he thrust back in, and they pulsed faster, harder, as if responding to the desperation in my voice.

"The ridges," I panted. "They're—"

"Reading you," he said, setting a rhythm that was already driving me insane. "Learning what you like. They'll move faster when you're close. I can't control it, can't stop it—"

The greenskin tendrils wrapped around my thighs, my waist, creating pressure and friction everywhere at once. One strand brushed across my nipple and I nearly came from that alone.

"Touch yourself," he commanded. "I want to feel you clench around me when you come."

My hand slid between us, finding my clit, and the ridges inside me immediately responded—pulsing faster, harder, as if they could sense how close I was. The greenskin tightened around us both, the strands moving like sea-grass in a current, brushing and teasing until I couldn't think, couldn't breathe—

"Rainse—I'm—"

"That's it. Come for me."

The orgasm slammed into me, and the ridges went wild —moving in rapid waves that prolonged the pleasure until I was sobbing his name. Through it all, I felt the greenskin trembling against my skin, felt it tighten around him as he followed me over with a shout.

The ridges pulsed one final time as he emptied himself inside me, and the greenskin flared so bright it turned the whole hut blue-green.

When I could think again, I was trembling and definitely crying.

"That was—" My voice broke. "The ridges—"

"I know." He was shaking too, pressing kisses to my face, my throat, anywhere he could reach. "I felt it. Through the bond. What they were doing to you."

"That's not fair. You have a significant biological advantage."

He laughed breathlessly. "Are you complaining?"

"Absolutely not. I'm simply noting it for scientific accuracy." I ran my hand down his back, feeling the greenskin strands still trembling with aftershocks. "Though I may need additional data. For verification purposes."

"Scientist," he accused fondly.

"Yours," I corrected, and felt the bond pulse between us in agreement.

"As I said. You're the scientist. Conduct more trials if you're unsure."

I laughed, the sound fading into something quieter. "I felt it," I said. "The bond. During—I felt it."

"I know." His hand found mine, fingers lacing together. "So did I."

"Is it always like that?"

"I don't know." He turned toward me, propping his head on his hand. "I've never had a mate before. But according to my brothers, yes. It gets stronger every time."

"That seems dangerous."

"Extremely." His thumb traced circles on my palm. "Are you frightened?"

I considered that. Was I? This thing between us defied every logical framework I'd built my life around. It was alien and overwhelming and completely beyond my control.

"No," I said, surprising myself. "I'm not frightened. I'm just... glad."

"Glad?"

"That it's you." I met his eyes. "I didn't want this. Didn't ask for it. But if I had to be swept off a sinking boat and nearly eaten by a shark and marooned on an island with an alien who kidnapped me—"

"Rescued," he corrected.

"Kidnapped," I insisted. "If all of that had to happen, I'm glad it led me to you."

His expression did something complicated. "That might be the most romantic thing anyone's ever said to me."

"Really? I thought it was more of a backhanded compliment."

"I'll take what I can get." He pulled me closer, tucking me against his chest. The greenskin along his ribs curled around me like a living blanket, warm and comforting. "For what it's worth, I'm glad it's you too. Even if you do mock my people's cuisine."

"Seaweed pudding is not cuisine. It's a dare."

He laughed, the sound rumbling through his chest into mine. Outside, the storm was beginning to ease, the rain softening from a hammer to a whisper. Dawn wasn't far off—I could feel it in the way the darkness had started to thin at the edges.

"What happens now?" I asked quietly.

"Now we sleep," he said. "And in the morning, we'll figure out the rest."

"That's not very specific."

"You want a plan?"

"I'm a scientist. I always want a plan."

"All right." He pressed a kiss to my hair. "The plan is: we wake up. We go back to the main lodge. You submit a DNA sample to make the bond official in the eyes of the Hot Tatties agency. We tell my brothers. We probably get lectured by Pam. And then we start building a life together."

"Just like that?"

"Just like that."

I was quiet for a moment, letting the words settle. A life together. It should have terrified me. Instead, it felt like the first deep breath after surfacing from a long dive.

"Okay," I said.

"Okay?"

"Yes." I tilted my head up to kiss him, soft and sure. "Let's do that."

His smile was brighter than his greenskin. "You're sure?"

"I'm sure." I settled back against his chest, listening to the steady rhythm of his heartbeat. "Besides, someone needs to teach you proper scientific method. Consider it my contribution to intergalactic relations."

"Noble of you."

"I'm very noble. You're lucky to have me."

"I know," he said, and there was no humour in it—just quiet, devastating honesty.

We lay there as the storm died away and the first grey light of dawn crept through the gaps in the walls. My eyes were heavy, my body pleasantly exhausted, but I didn't want to sleep yet. Didn't want to miss a single moment of this strange, perfect peace.

"Rainse?"

"Mmm?"

"Thank you."

"For what?"

"For saving me." I pressed my palm flat against his chest, feeling the greenskin pulse beneath my touch. "Not just from the shark. From... everything else. From spending my whole life measuring the ocean instead of swimming in it."

His arms tightened around me. "You saved me too."

"From jellyfish. It's hardly comparable."

"Not from jellyfish," he said quietly. "From loneliness. From thinking I'd never be worthy of this. You gave me something I'd stopped believing in."

"What's that?"

"Hope."

My throat went tight. I didn't trust myself to speak, so I just held him tighter and let the sound of the ocean outside fill the silence.

When I finally did drift off, it was with his heartbeat steady beneath my ear and his greenskin glowing soft and warm around us both—a light in the darkness, guiding me home.

17

Rainse

The walk back to the main lodge felt surreal. I was holding my mate's hand—my actual, confirmed, *chosen* mate—and the morning sun was turning everything gold, and I couldn't stop grinning like an idiot.

Verity caught me at it. "You're doing it again."

"Doing what?"

"Looking insufferably pleased with yourself."

"I am insufferably pleased with myself," I said. "I have excellent reason."

She laughed, and the sound went straight through the bond into my chest. The greenskin along my shoulders shivered in response, and her eyes tracked the movement with scientific interest that was somehow also hungry.

"We should probably look less..." She gestured vaguely at us. "Obvious."

"We look like two people who spent the night in a hut during a storm."

"We look like two people who spent the night *fucking* in a hut during a storm," she corrected. "There's a difference."

"Is there? I'm not familiar with human social cues."

"Liar." But she was smiling, her hair still damp and tangled, her lips still faintly swollen from kissing. She looked thoroughly ravished, and I was absolutely not sorry about it.

We crested the path, and the main lodge came into view. A few early risers were already moving around—staff preparing breakfast, a finman doing morning stretches on the beach, two human women chatting over coffee on the terrace.

They all stopped and stared.

"Subtle," Verity muttered.

"Perhaps we should have combed your hair."

"Perhaps you should have dimmed your greenskin. It's still glowing."

I glanced down. She was right—faint traces of bioluminescence still clung to the strands along my ribs and shoulders, the aftereffects of bonding. "I can't control that."

"Convenient excuse."

"Scientific fact," I countered, and she elbowed me in the ribs.

We made it halfway across the main deck before Fionn appeared in our path, arms folded, expression somewhere between amused and exasperated. Elise stood beside him, looking delighted.

"There you are," Fionn said mildly. "We were starting to wonder if the storm had washed you out to sea."

"We took shelter," I said.

"I can see that." His gaze flicked between us, taking in every detail—our wrinkled clothes, the faint glow of my greenskin, the way Verity's hand was still tucked in mine. "Productive shelter, I assume."

"Very," Verity said before I could answer, and I loved her for it.

Elise practically bounced on her toes. "Oh my God. You bonded. You actually bonded. Fionn, they bonded!"

"I have eyes, love."

"This is so exciting! Welcome to the family, Verity. Officially. Well, almost officially. You need to do the DNA test, right? But basically officially. Close enough." She grabbed Verity's free hand. "How are you feeling? Are you okay? Do you need anything? Water? Food? A nap?"

"I need," Verity said carefully, "to submit a DNA sample and then possibly sleep for twelve hours."

"We can arrange that," Fionn said. "Though Pam will want to speak with you first."

I groaned. "Can't that wait?"

"You vanished for an entire night with a human female during a tropical storm," Fionn said. "No, it cannot wait. She's already called twice."

Verity squeezed my hand. "It's fine. Let's just get it over with."

Twenty minutes later, we were seated in Fionn's office —a human conference room that had been converted into something resembling a command centre. Pam's hologram flickered to life above the desk, her expression the particular blend of professional and long-suffering that I'd come to know well.

"Rainse," she said. "And Verity. How lovely to see you both alive and well."

"Thank you for your concern," I said.

"That wasn't concern. That was sarcasm." She adjusted her glasses. "Now, would someone like to explain to me why you two disappeared? Again? During a storm?"

Verity's cheeks flushed pink. I bit back a smile.

"We took shelter from the storm," I said.

"I'm sure you did." Pam's gaze sharpened.

"Yes, we did" Verity confirmed. "And I'd now like to submit a DNA sample to confirm the match officially."

Pam's expression softened slightly. "I see. And this was your choice? You weren't coerced or pressured?"

"Absolutely not." Verity's voice was firm. "Rainse has been nothing but respectful. Well, mostly respectful. The point is, I chose this. I want this."

Something in my chest loosened at her words. I'd known she wanted me—the bond made that clear—but hearing her say it out loud, in front of witnesses, felt like vindication.

"Very well," Pam said. "Elise has been kind enough to offer the *Tidebound* to fly the sample to our lab. That will make everything much quicker. Paul, my representative on the island, will give you a sample pack. All you have to do is spit in a tube, nothing scary. If you do it right away, then results should be back within twenty-four hours."

"Twenty-four hours?" I echoed. "That fast?"

"I'm fast-tracking it." Pam's mouth twitched. "Consider it a gesture of goodwill. Or perhaps an attempt to prevent any more unauthorised glowing huts on my island. Yes, Fionn told me."

I worked hard to repress a comment along the lines of 'my greenskin is none of your business'.

"Verity, we'll also need to discuss your status moving forward. You came here as a rescued shipwreck victim, but if you're choosing to stay—"

"I have questions about that," Verity interrupted. "If I stay, what happens to my work? My research?"

Pam raised an eyebrow. "What would you like to happen?"

"I'm a marine biologist," Verity said. "Specifically, I study cetaceans—whales, dolphins, that sort of thing. I've spent years building my career, and I'm not willing to give that up. Not even for—" She glanced at me. "Well. Not even for excellent reasons. I can do some of my work remotely, but I need a lab. Storage for samples. Assistants or students."

Pride surged through me. This was my mate—brilliant, determined, unwilling to compromise herself for anyone. I didn't want her to give up her work, her passion for me. I would support her in her endeavours, no matter what.

"We could establish a research position here," Fionn said thoughtfully. "The island is well-positioned for cetacean studies. And having a legitimate marine biologist on staff would help maintain our cover as a private resort for the rich."

"That could work," Verity said slowly. "I'd need access to equipment—hydrophones, tagging supplies, a boat for field work. And I'd want to publish my findings, which means collaborating with other researchers."

"We can arrange all of that," Pam said. "Within reason, of course. You'd need to be careful about what information you share. No accidental references to alien mermen in your papers."

"I'm a scientist," Verity said dryly. "I know how to keep my work and my personal life separate."

"There's another option," I said, an idea forming. "You could study us."

Everyone turned to look at me.

"Explain," Pam said.

"Verity is a biologist who studies marine life," I said. "We are marine life. Alien marine life that humanity doesn't know exists. The data she could gather—about our physiology, our adaptation to Earth's oceans, the biological basis of the mate bond—it would be groundbreaking."

Verity's eyes had gone wide. "That's... actually brilliant. I'd need to shift my focus from cetaceans to something more interdisciplinary—marine biology meets xenobiology, essentially. But the core skills are transferable. And the research questions are fascinating. How do finfolk navigate? What's the evolutionary purpose of greenskin? Why are you biologically compatible with humans when you evolved on a completely different planet?"

"You're getting excited," I observed.

"I'm a scientist. This is the opportunity of a lifetime." She turned to Pam. "Would that be allowed? Studying the finfolk?"

"With appropriate ethical oversight and consent from the subjects, yes," Pam said. "In fact, having documented research on finfolk biology could be invaluable for future matches. I might even be able to get some extra funding from the Intergalactic University. We know remarkably little about the scientific basis for the mate bond."

"I could change that," Verity said, and I could see her mind already racing ahead, planning studies and forming hypotheses.

"Then it's settled," Fionn said. "Verity will stay on as the island's resident marine biologist and xenobiologist. We'll provide whatever equipment and support she needs."

"There's one more thing," Verity said, her hand finding mine again. "The *Minerva*. My team. They're expecting me to contact them with a decision about returning to the ship."

The joy that had been building in my chest dimmed slightly. "What will you tell them?"

She was quiet for a moment, considering. "The truth. Or as much of it as I can share. That I've been offered a research position too good to pass up, studying marine life in a private facility. They won't be happy—I'm supposed to be on that expedition for another six weeks —but they'll understand. Science is full of people following unexpected opportunities."

"And if they don't understand?" I asked quietly.

"Then they don't." She met my eyes. "I'm choosing this, Rainse. I'm choosing you, and this island, and the chance to study something no human has ever studied before. If that costs me some professional relationships, I'll rebuild. I'm good at what I do."

The bond pulsed with her certainty, and I had to resist the urge to kiss her right there in front of everyone.

"Excellent," Pam said. "Then let's get that DNA sample processed."

Verity stood, then paused. "Actually, one more question. What happens during these twenty-four hours? Before the results come back?"

"You're free to spend time together," Pam said. "Just perhaps avoid any more mysterious glowing huts. The staff are starting to ask questions."

After Verity had submitted her sample, she stifled a yawn. "Sorry. The adrenaline is wearing off."

"Food first," Fionn said. "Then sleep. You both look dead on your feet."

We made our way to the dining area, where the breakfast service was in full swing. The smell of fresh bread and coffee filled the air, mixing with the salt breeze from the ocean. Several finfolk and humans were scattered across the tables, and I felt their curious gazes tracking us as we entered.

"Everyone's staring," Verity murmured.

"Let them," I said. "They'll have to get used to seeing us together."

We claimed a table near the windows, and within moments, a server appeared with coffee for Verity and water for me. I ordered enough food for both of us—fruit, bread, eggs prepared three different ways, and a dish of raw fish that made Verity wrinkle her nose.

"You're actually going to eat that?" she asked.

"It's breakfast."

"It's... still moving."

"It's fresh."

She shuddered. "I'm going to have to watch you eat raw fish regularly, aren't I?"

"I'm afraid so. Unless you'd like to try it?"

"Absolutely not."

I smiled and took a bite, enjoying the way she deliberately looked away. "You study marine life but won't eat it raw?"

"I study marine life *because* I respect it," she said. "Eating it raw feels like a betrayal of that respect."

"Even though you eat it cooked?"

"That's different. Cooking is... civilised."

"And we're not?"

Her gaze flicked to me, warm and knowing. "Oh, you're many things, Rainse. Civilised might not be at the top of the list."

The bond hummed with shared amusement and something deeper—affection, desire, the promise of what we'd shared in the hut. My greenskin rippled in response.

"Behave," she murmured. "We're in public."

"I am behaving."

"Your greenskin is glowing again."

"That's not something I can control."

"Convenient."

Before I could respond, Cerban's voice carried across the dining area. "Well, well. What do we have here?"

I looked up to find my clutch-brother approaching, Maelis tucked against his side. They both wore matching grins—the kind that promised teasing and embarrassment in equal measure.

"Cerban," I said warily. "Maelis."

"Rainse." Cerban pulled out a chair without invitation, settling in across from us. "I heard an interesting rumour this morning. Something about mysterious lights on the north beach?"

"We took shelter from the storm," I said.

"I'm sure you did." His grin widened. "Very thorough shelter, from what I understand."

Maelis elbowed him. "Be nice." She turned to Verity, offering a genuine smile. "Hi. I'm Maelis, and this is my insufferable mate, Cerban. Welcome to the island. And congratulations."

"Thank you," Verity said, seeming relieved by the friendly greeting. "I'm Verity. And yes, before anyone asks, we're mates. The DNA test is being processed now, but for us that is just a formality."

"Smart," Maelis said. "Get ahead of the gossip. Trust me, on an island this small, everyone knows everything within about six hours."

"Five hours," Cerban corrected. "I timed it once."

"You did not."

"I absolutely did. Remember when we-"

"This is not the time." Maelis rolled her eyes but was smiling. She turned back to Verity. "So, marine biologist?"

"That's right. I study cetaceans—whales and dolphins, mostly. Or I did. Now I'm thinking about expanding into xenobiology."

"Studying us, you mean?" Cerban's expression shifted to something more interested. "That could be useful. We still don't fully understand why the mate bond works with humans."

"That would be one of my research questions," Verity said, warming to the topic. "The biological compatibility between species that evolved on completely different planets—it shouldn't work. But it does. Rainse mentioned that the dating agency works with other alien species, not just finfolk. Why? What's the mechanism? Is it something in your DNA that happens to align with ours? Or is there something more complex happening?"

"You're going to fit right in," Maelis said. "I'm a scuba diver, so I can't help much with the biology side, but if you ever need someone to collect samples or map underwater caves, I'm your person."

"Noted. Thank you." Verity glanced at me. "Shall we go and have a nap?"

"Yes. As soon as I have had another portion of this fish. It almost tastes like back home."

I felt Cerban's eyes on me, assessing. When Verity turned to respond to something Maelis said, he leaned forward slightly.

"You did it," he said quietly. "You found your mate."

"I did."

"How does it feel?"

I considered the question. How did it feel? Like everything had finally clicked into place. Like the loneliness that had haunted me since the Matriarchs' judgement had been washed away. Like I'd found the piece of myself I hadn't known was missing.

"Like drowning and breathing at the same time," I said finally.

Cerban smiled—a real smile, full of understanding. "Yes. Exactly like that."

After breakfast, Verity's exhaustion finally caught up with her. I walked her back to her room—a well-appointed bungalow high up on the hill, with windows that overlooked the water.

"You should rest," I said, though leaving her felt physically painful. The bond pulled at me, wanting me to stay close.

"Are you giving me orders now?" she asked, but there was no heat in it.

"I'm expressing concern for your wellbeing."

"Mmm." She swayed slightly, and I caught her elbow. "Okay, fine. Maybe I'm more tired than I thought. That hut didn't exactly have the world's most comfortable sleeping arrangements."

"We weren't doing much sleeping," I pointed out.

"True." She looked up at me, eyes soft despite her exhaustion. "Will you stay? Just until I fall asleep?"

The question hit me harder than it should have. "Of course."

Inside, the room was cool and quiet, the bed large and inviting. Verity kicked off her shoes and collapsed onto it with a grateful sigh.

"This is so much better than sand and cushions," she mumbled into the pillow.

I sat on the edge of the bed, running my hand down her back. The greenskin along my arm reached out instinctively, the strands brushing against her shirt in a gentle rhythm.

"Your greenskin does that a lot," she said drowsily. "The reaching thing. Is it conscious?"

"No. I have no control over it. It just... wants to touch you. To maintain the connection. I don't think my brothers' greenskin does it. But..."

"I like it." Her eyes were already closing. "It feels safe."

Safe. Such a simple word, but it meant everything.

I stayed there, hand on her back, greenskin maintaining that gentle contact, until her breathing evened out into sleep. Even then, I didn't want to leave. The bond was content, settled, humming with satisfaction at her nearness.

But I had things to do. Preparations to make. A life to build with her.

I pressed a kiss to her temple and whispered, "Twenty-four hours. Then you're officially mine."

She smiled in her sleep, and the bond pulsed with shared contentment.

18

Verity

I woke to sunlight streaming through the windows and Rainse's greenskin wrapped around me like a living blanket. For a disorienting moment, I couldn't remember where I was—then everything came rushing back. The storm. The hut. The bonding. The DNA test.

The results.

"You're thinking very loudly," Rainse murmured against my hair.

"What time is it?"

"Early. The sun's barely up." His arms tightened around me. "Nervous?"

"Should I be?"

"No." He pressed a kiss to my shoulder. "The test will only confirm what we already know."

"And what's that?"

"That you're mine. That I'm yours. That the universe got something right for once."

I turned in his arms to face him. His eyes were still soft with sleep, his hair mussed, greenskin moving in lazy patterns across his skin. Beautiful. Alien. Mine.

"When will we know?" I asked.

"Fionn said the *Tidebound* returned late last night. The lab processes samples overnight. So..." He glanced at the window, calculating. "Any time now, actually."

My stomach flipped. "That's—"

His strange alien watch chimed from his right wrist.

We both froze.

"That could be anything," I said.

"It could," he agreed, but he was already reaching for it.

The screen lit up with a message from Pam: *Results are in. Call me in one hour.*

"One hour," I repeated. "That's... not much time."

"Enough for a shower," Rainse said, already pulling me out of bed. "And breakfast. And possibly a moment of panic."

"I don't panic."

"Scientist," he said fondly. "You've been fidgeting since you woke up."

"That's not panic. That's excited anticipation."

"Is there a difference?"

"Scientifically speaking, yes. Panic involves elevated cortisol levels and—" I stopped when I saw his expression. "You're teasing me."

"I am." He kissed me, slow and thorough. "Now shower. We have results to collect."

Fifty-three minutes later, we stood outside Pam's office. I'd changed into clean clothes—Maelis had given them to me, as she was closest to me in size—and attempted to do something with my hair. Rainse looked infuriatingly composed, though his greenskin was shimmering more than usual.

"Ready?" he asked.

"No. Yes. I don't know." I took a breath. "This is ridiculous. We know what the results will say."

"Then there's nothing to worry about."

"Then why are you glowing?"

"Anticipation," he said. "Not panic."

I laughed despite myself. "Okay. Let's do this."

The door opened before we could knock. Fionn stood there, looking far too entertained.

"Come in," he said. "Pam's standing by on holo."

Inside, Elise occupied one of the visitor chairs. Cerban and Maelis had somehow appeared as well, crowded onto the small sofa.

"This isn't a spectator sport," I said.

"It absolutely is," Cerban replied. "We've been waiting for this."

"Waiting for what? Me to be proven scientifically compatible with your brother?"

"Waiting for Rainse to finally stop being miserable," Maelis said gently. "Trust me, he's been insufferable."

Rainse shot her a look but didn't argue.

Fionn activated the holo projector, and Pam's image flickered to life above the desk. She looked immaculate as always, though there was something almost warm in her expression.

"Good morning," she said. "I assume you're all assembled to hear the results?"

"We are," Fionn confirmed.

Pam pulled up a holographic display that materialised in the centre of the room. Data streamed across the screen—complex genetic sequences, compatibility percentages, biological markers I only half understood.

"The results are conclusive," she said without preamble. "Verity Walsh and Rainse of Eynhallow are a genetic match. The compatibility rating is exceptionally high even for Hot Tatties algorithm standards."

The room erupted. Elise actually squealed. Cerban clapped Rainse on the shoulder hard enough to make him stagger. Maelis was grinning so widely I thought her face might split.

I just stood there, staring at the data.

"That's..." I couldn't find words.

"Remarkable," Pam finished. "Yours is among the highest compatibility ratings we've ever recorded."

"What does that mean?" Rainse asked, his hand finding mine.

"It means the bond will be exceptionally strong. More resilient, more intuitive. You'll be able to sense each other across greater distances, respond to each other's emotions more acutely." Pam's expression softened further. "It means you're very, very well matched."

"Told you," Rainse murmured, and the smug satisfaction in his voice made me want to kiss him and strangle him in equal measure.

"Congratulations," Fionn said warmly. "Both of you. This calls for celebration."

"It calls for paperwork," Pam corrected, but she was smiling. "Verity, you'll need to update your status with the Intergalactic Authority. You're now officially recognised as a finman's mate, which grants you certain protections and privileges. You'll also need to decide on residency—"

"I'm staying here," I said. "On the island. For my research."

"Excellent. I'm sure Elise will let you use the *Tidebound* for your move. If not, the agency can arrange it."

"Moving," I muttered. It suddenly all seemed so real. And I was ready for it.

I looked at Rainse. His greenskin was glowing properly now, bright enough to cast blue-green shadows on the walls. The bond hummed between us, stronger than ever, pulsing with shared joy.

The rest of the morning dissolved into celebration. Someone—probably Elise—had arranged an impromptu party on the beach. Tables laden with food, drinks cooling in ice buckets, other finfolk and humans already gathering when word spread.

"This is too much," I protested as we emerged into sunshine and noise.

"This is exactly right," Fionn said. "We don't get many mate bonds confirmed. Let us celebrate."

What followed was a blur of congratulations and well-wishes. Finfolk I'd never met touched my shoulder in greeting. Humans welcomed me with hugs. The kitchen staff brought out dish after dish—some human, some finfolk, some fascinating fusion of both.

Through it all, Rainse stayed close, his hand in mine or his greenskin brushing against my arm. The bond pulsed steadily, anchoring me when the attention became overwhelming.

"Okay?" he murmured during a brief lull.

"Yes. Just... a lot of people."

"We can leave if you want. Go somewhere quiet."

I looked around at the smiling faces, the joy that seemed to radiate from everyone. "Give me five more minutes. Then yes, please."

Those five minutes stretched to twenty, but eventually we managed to slip away. The crowd had thinned anyway, people drifting back to their various pursuits, and no one seemed to notice when we disappeared down the beach path.

We walked in comfortable silence until the sounds of the party faded behind us, replaced by the steady rhythm of waves. The afternoon sun painted everything gold.

"Better?" Rainse asked.

"Much." I squeezed his hand. "Though I think your brothers are planning something. Cerban had that look."

"They're always planning something. Usually it involves embarrassing me."

"I look forward to it."

He laughed, and we kept walking until we reached a quiet stretch of beach, sheltered by rocks on one side and palm trees on the other. The sand here was pristine, unmarked by footprints.

Rainse stopped and turned to face me, both hands finding mine. His greenskin shimmered in the afternoon light, and I could feel the bond thrumming between us—stronger now, more certain.

"We're official," he said.

"Scientifically verified," I agreed. "I'm your mate. You're stuck with me."

"Stuck," he repeated, smiling. "That's one way to put it."

"How would you put it?"

He was quiet for a moment, his thumbs tracing circles on the backs of my hands. "Blessed. Lucky. Grateful beyond measure."

My throat went tight. "That's very poetic."

"You bring it out in me." He pulled me closer. "I spent mooncrossings thinking I'd never have this. That I wasn't worthy of it. And then you fell into my ocean."

"Technically I was thrown into your ocean by a whale."

"Best thing that whale ever did."

I laughed, slightly watery. "We should probably thank it."

"We will. Once you track it down for your research." His expression grew more serious. "Verity, I know this happened fast. A week ago, you didn't know aliens existed. Now you're bonded to one, moving to a remote island, changing your entire life—"

"Stop," I interrupted gently. "I know what I'm doing. Yes, it's fast. Yes, it's crazy. But it's also right." I pressed my palm flat against his chest, feeling the steady beat of his heart and the responsive shiver of his greenskin. "The bond isn't forcing me to stay. I'm choosing it. I'm choosing you."

"Even with all the complications?"

"Especially with them." I smiled. "I'm a scientist. I love complications. They make life interesting."

"You make my life interesting," he said quietly. "You make it worth living."

The bond pulsed with the depth of his emotion, and I felt it echo in my own chest. This thing between us—it was more than biology, more than chemistry. It was choice and commitment and the promise of building something together.

"Kiss me," I said.

He didn't need to be told twice.

His mouth found mine, soft and sure. The kiss tasted of salt air and new beginnings. His greenskin wrapped around us both, glowing faintly in the bright daylight, and I felt the bond settle—content, certain, home.

When we finally broke apart, both slightly breathless, the sun had begun its descent toward the horizon.

"So," Rainse said, his forehead resting against mine. "What now?"

"Now?" I tilted my head back to look at him. "Now we start building our life. Together."

"Just like that?"

"Just like that." I kissed him again, quick and light. "One day at a time. One discovery at a time. One moment at a time."

"I can work with that," he murmured.

We stood there as the afternoon mellowed into evening, the ocean singing its eternal song around us. And for the first time since the whale had capsized my boat and thrown me into impossible circumstances, I felt completely, perfectly at peace.

This was where I was meant to be.

With him.

Always.

All three mermen have found their match - but there are more aliens waiting for mates! If you haven't already, take a look at the Starlight Highlanders *and* Starlight Vikings *series, both set in the same world and involving the Hot Tatties dating agency.*

Subscribe to my newsletter for the latest updates as well as lots of cute cat pictures:
skyemackinnon.com/newsletter

Want to know more about Ma'vel and Jonet, the couple whose union was described in the Archives? Read the prequel to the series, Ma'vel, *set in 17th century Scotland, for free!*
skyemackinnon.com/mavel

THE STARLIGHT UNIVERSE

This book is part of the Starlight Universe, an entire galaxy filled with hunky aliens, exotic planets, and the human women ready to find love among the stars.

Starlight Highlanders Mail Order Brides

Alien Highlanders in kilts come to Earth in search of brides... and take them to planet Albya. Three m/f standalones full of humour, action and steamy romance. Part of the Intergalactic Dating Agency.

Starlight Vikings

Set on Earth and on the spaceship Valkyr, this trilogy of m/f standalones is all about hunky alien Vikings in need of females. Part of the Intergalactic Dating Agency.

Starlight Mermen

Hundreds of years ago, they crash-landed on Earth and gave rise to many of our legends. Now, they're back, desperate for female mates. Part of the Intergalactic Dating Agency.

The Intergalactic Guide to Humans

A humorous take on alien abductions, probing and other shenanigans. One reverse harem trilogy about clueless aliens and the human woman they abducted, followed by several standalone romances with various pairings (m/f, f/m/f and m/m). If you want light entertainment filled with unicorns, fabulous misunderstandings and unusual body parts, this is the series for you.

Starlight Monsters

These aliens are not your usual humanoids... they have claws, fangs, tails, scales, knotty dicks and will growl at you. Interconnected m/f standalones with lots of action, steam and fated mates.

Skye MacKinnon is a Scottish romance author who was raised by elves in the mystical Highlands and calls the Loch Ness monster her friend. Her bestselling books weave together romance with action, suspense and whimsical humour, creating page-turners filled with strong heroines, alpha heroes and loveable monsters.

Whether she's writing about aliens in kilts, hunky Vikings or cat shifter assassins, Skye likes to put a new spin on familiar tropes. Some of her heroines don't have to choose, some fall in love with other women, and others get abducted by clueless aliens.

Skye lives with her bossy cat on the west coast of Scotland and uses the dramatic views from her office as an inspiration, no matter whether she writes fantasy, paranormal or science fiction romance. Until she gets abducted by aliens, that is.

Subscribe to her newsletter:

skyemackinnon.com/newsletter

- **Between Rebels** (sci-fi reverse harem set in the Planet Athion shared world)
- **The Mars Diaries** (sci-fi reverse harem)
- **Aliens and Animals** (f/f sci-fi romance co-written with Arizona Tape)

Paranormal & Fantasy Romance

- **Claiming Her Bears** (post-apocalyptic shifter reverse harem)
- **Daughter of Winter** (fantasy reverse harem)
- **Catnip Assassins** (urban fantasy reverse harem)
- **Infernal Descent** (paranormal reverse harem based on Dante's Inferno, co-written with Bea Paige)
- **Seven Wardens** (fantasy reverse harem co-written with Laura Greenwood)
- **The Lost Siren** (post-apocalyptic, paranormal reverse harem co-written with Liza Street)

Other Series

- **Academy of Time** (time travel academy standalones, reverse harem and m/f)
- **Defiance** (contemporary reverse harem with a hint of thriller/suspense)

Standalones

- Song of Souls – m/f fantasy romance, fairy tale retelling
- Highland Butterflies – sapphic romance
- Wings of Time and Fate - epic fantasy

Box Sets

- Daggers & Destiny – a fantasy romance starter library
- Stars & Seduction - a science fiction romance starter library

Buy your books direct from the author

GET 20% OFF YOUR NEXT EBOOK OR AUDIOBOOK!

USE CODE BOOKWORMS AT SKYEMACKINNON.COM/SHOP

EBOOKS, AUDIOBOOKS, PRINT BOOKS, MERCHANDISE & MORE

www.ingramcontent.com/pod-product-compliance
Lightning Source LLC
Chambersburg PA
CBHW060546190726
48283CB00003B/886